My chair was next to a round table covered with a chenille cloth. On it stood a silver dish, tall with a stem and a solid base. I think its name is a tazza. It was filled with a mouth-watering collection of bonbons and sweets.

The first sweet I ate was marzipan. I was very hungry.

"Take your fill," a masculine voice said. To me it might have been Jehovah! I rose and turned to the newcomer.

He was tall and good looking. Black hair and gray eyes. "Take them," he said again.

"No, thank you, sir. I should not have fallen a prey to temptation—"

"It's nothing. Please don't give it another thought."

Later, in the street, I passed through the crowds without seeing them. I believed I had fallen in love. And I did not know his name.

THE
LOVING
HEART

Mollie Chappell

FAWCETT CREST • NEW YORK

THE LOVING HEART

THIS BOOK CONTAINS THE COMPLETE TEXT OF THE ORIGINAL HARDCOVER EDITION.

Published by Fawcett Crest Books, a unit of CBS Publications, the Consumer Publishing Division of CBS Inc., by arrangement with William Collins Sons & Company Ltd.

Copyright © 1977 by Mollie Chappell

ISBN: 0-449-23991-8

Printed in the United States of America

10   9   8   7   6   5   4   3   2   1

One

My name is Martha Bates. I am eighteen years old and it is the evening of the day my aunt Dorcas was buried. I loved Dorcas more than anyone else in the world. She was my world. She was goodness and kindness to me. I am an orphan and have no living relations now that Dorcas is dead.

I must leave the village where I have always lived and go out and face the world and make a living there. I am frightened at the prospect because the world can be a cruel place for a girl on her own with little money, and I have very little money. The house we lived in and where Dorcas had her school was rented from Farmer Gregson and I know he wants it for his son. I could not carry on the school, anyway, because at the end of her life my aunt had to close it since she was too ill to carry on. Many times, when she lay suffering,

I hoped she could not tell how impatient the farmer was to get his property back.

When he met me in the village street and asked after my aunt, he did not go so far as to say, "If she is going to die, tell her to hurry up. My son needs that house." I just had the feeling this was what he would have liked to say.

So, as I have said, I must leave there and go out into the world. But if I am frightened now, how frightened Dorcas must have been, and many times, for there was little money and perhaps she wondered how she would keep me, a tall, strong girl with a healthy appetite. I earned nothing.

I am afraid my name, Martha Bates, suits the way I look for it has a turnip ring and I am a country girl. Pink cheeks, bright eyes, good strong teeth, excellent health. Yet beneath all this I am pure romantic. I have longed to be called Adela or even Martha with the French spelling. *Marthe*. Dorcas would have none of it. "Be yourself," she ordered. "Then you will always know where you are going."

When I was old enough, I helped her with the little ones in the school. They were a noisy, lovable crew. I taught them their letters and numbers, and songs and simple verses.

The older girls were the daughters of local tradesmen whose mothers wished them to have a smear of learning and some good manners. Dorcas would have taught them more but they did not wish to be bluestockings. Enough to be able to read a romantic tale, write a letter, add up a bill to make certain they were not cheated. Richer parents sent their girls off to boarding schools which were becoming fashionable.

Dorcas's pupils were scrambling up the bottom of the social ladder hereabouts.

The social ladder. Jacob's ladder to heaven was not as important!

The Catechism which I learned so diligently tells us to do our duty in that state of life unto which it pleased God to call us. But I think this strict directive applies only to the poor and the vast army of workers. It is what God and their neighbours here on earth expect for *them*, and they had better mind they stay there! Their superiors in health and brain, with money and good fortune, are admired when they forge ahead and clamber out of that state they were born in into a better and richer and more comfortable life. This is considered what God put us on earth for, to compete and win and better ourselves. But why not all of us?

It is the year 1860, nearly a decade after the Great Exhibition, and as if that waved the flag for us and said, "Keep on. You are doing well," our country is borne along on a wave of prosperity. Nothing seems to stop us from becoming the richest and most powerful of countries. Fortunes are made, life smiles on the energetic and the forceful and the man with the touch for money-making. But everyone cannot make money. Not everyone is placed to make it and—and here I come back to my vexed questioning of the justice of things— if you are poor, you seem to be blamed for it. If you do not get the chance to work, it is your fault.

Here in our village, conventions are as rigid as an iron corset. Dorcas and I curtsey to Lady Ann, who is higher born than the squire and whose cold face reminds you of it, but in turn Dorcas expects to be treated as deferentially by her inferiors. "Why is it correct," I asked her, "for the squire to invite the doctor to dine but not the doctor's wife? The rector may dine at the Hall but a glass of sherry is all the curate gets, and back to his lodgings! Surely," I said, "God in His mercy has enough to do with tormented climbing boys under cruel sweep-masters, boys scaring crows in the fields from four in the morning, all week, for fourpence a week, servant girls learning to be slaves on three pounds a year—"

Dorcas agreed these were iniquities. But I expect she, the kindest of women, also thought they were the order of things.

Someone should lead a crusade, I thought stormily. Lead the young and the poor and the hopeless. Then perhaps the fish-eyed Lady Ann would not have her natural conceit fed by making a hungry curate feel worse!

Still, I loved my timid aunt dearly, and forgave her. If there was such a crusade, I knew I would excuse her from joining. It would be very much against her nature to do it. My mother died after I was born. My father died three months before I was born. So Dorcas brought me up.

One morning Sarah came to tell me that my aunt had died in her sleep. I knelt beside the bed and could only pray that now she was in heaven she would find peace and rest from the burdens she had shouldered so uncomplainingly here on earth.

It rained, the day of the funeral. November is usually a wet month. The rector spoke the funeral service in the way he preached, as if he was doing us a favour by being God's messenger. The rector always gave the impression that heaven too was graded socially. There,

there were armies of working angels ready to wait eternally upon the likes of him and the squire Lady Ann. How else could it be?

As I thought this, I saw the feather on her ladyship's bonnet quiver as a sign to the rector that she was bored with the sermon and he must finish.

After Dorcas's funeral, only Sarah and I returned to the house. Neighbours who had come to the churchyard hurried home from the rain. "Make tea," I told Sarah, "and bring it into the parlour. We will drink it there together."

She brought it in on the silver tray and with what I called the "company cups", cups of egg-shell thin china which had been my aunt's pride. The parlour was almost denuded of furniture for I had been selling what I could, all the time since Dorcas's death, getting little for it because people knew I had to sell and drove a hard bargain.

I did not mind though I needed money. All I wanted was to leave here and find somewhere where I could begin a new life. I could not have stayed hereabouts where I would constantly be reminded of what life had once been.

Sarah had said she would get the carter to take what was left into Maidstone, and said she might go with him to see what she called "fair play". I thanked her and said that when I was settled in London I would write her, giving my address. "What shall I do with the china and linen?" she said.

"I would like to keep the silver tray," I said. "And teapot. And the company cups. If you want the linen, take it."

She nodded and said it would be useful and said she

would keep the tray and the cups safe until I got married. And the teapot. "Your bottom drawer," she said. "Your wedding chest."

"The books, Sarah. Dorcas's books. Could you find somewhere for them? I will pay, if I have to."

She nodded. I wondered what I would do without her, and thought what a strong right arm she must have been to Dorcas. More help than I had ever been. But I would not say so.

I said, "What are you going to do now?"

Her black eyes slitted as they did when she was amused. "Take my choice of the ladies who have been after me for a long time to work for them," Sarah said.

"Which ladies?"

"Your aunt's dearest friends. For years they have been at me, behind her back, to leave here and go to them, offering me more than she could afford to pay. 'Your loyalty does you credit, Sarah,' they would say. 'But I am certain Miss Dorcas would understand.' I am certain she would. But that is not my way. I do not think," Sarah said, "I shall put as my first choice she who kept whispering, as she left the sick room, 'When your mistress dies, Sarah, you come straight to me.' I would not care to have her as my employer if I were sick and ill."

It shocked me. I did not know friends behave thus. I did not wish to know their names, these ladies who had visited Dorcas here and drunk from the "company cups", and with jealous eyes watched Sarah as she went about her duties. Everyone in the village knew what a good servant Sarah Prendergast was.

"You will learn," I heard her say. "When you have flown the nest, you will learn there are vultures as well as sparrows out there! Fine feathers don't make anything except a greedy deceitful woman a greedy sight! You can buy anything if you have money."

They did not buy you, I thought.

She said it made her laugh to see them connive the one against the other. "They knew one another. It was only your sweet aunt who did not understand. If she had known, she would have tried to make me leave and accept more money."

She did not say *Miss Martha*, now. But I would not mention it. If she thought we were almost equals, she was wrong. I felt a fledgling chick beside Sarah with her cynicism and her knowledge of people and their ways. If I had to learn to be in some way like her, let me learn fast, I thought. For it did not seem as if the Golden Rule Dorcas had lived by and had tried to teach me would be of much use out in the world.

But, *"I shall not be a governess,"* I heard myself say with spirit. "I would rather die."

"Forget that talk," she told me. "No one would rather die, and dying from starvation must be a terrible death. I have seen people close to it and it is idle to say, 'I would rather die.' You will learn, anyway, that people do not die when perhaps they might wish to die, when things go wrong. To teach is better than to starve."

"No. I will dressmake, first. Or make bonnets."

I was handy with my needle. I enjoyed sewing and making bonnets. My bonnets were, I knew, the prettiest in the village. I expect Lady Ann thought them most unsuitable. Dressmakers and milliners, I told myself, might not be far up in the social scale but neither were governesses who only clung to their social posi-

tion by the skin of their teeth! I would prefer to be a
happy milliner. "I have enough money to go to London," I said. "I shall find work within a week."

"In a wash-leather bag, upstairs," I heard my companion say "there are eighteen sovereigns. They are
yours. Each birthday, your aunt put one sovereign by.
When you had your twenty-first birthday, she meant to
give them to you. There were times, I know, when she
went without to save the sovereign. But she never
missed. God rest her," Sarah said. "She was the best
lady I knew."

I rubbed the tears off my cheeks. Then I thought of
eighteen gold sovereigns, a fortune to me at this moment. I was rescued in the nick of time, I thought,
from near penury. I wished Dorcas was alive so that I
might embrace and kiss her as I used to do. On my
birthday, when she would give me some gift, a pretty
dress she had made secretly for me, a shawl she had
bought; in my pleasure I would put my arms around
her small waist and lift her into the air, so small was
she, so frail. She would laugh and protest and say,
"Put me down, Martha. What if a pupil came in? You
look as if you would put me to sit on top of the schoolroom cupboard and I will look like an owl nesting
there."

Dorcas was never happier than when she made others happy. But I would never kiss nor hug her again
nor lift her off her feet. I was learning that the deep
cruelty of loss is the thrust of the heart of memory.
"What about you, Sarah?" I said "If there is money
owing on your wages, I will pay it."

She said fiercely, "Did you think there would be

money owing?" No, I told myself. Dorcas would go without herself, rather than owe Sarah her wages.

Then we sat silent, both thinking of Dorcas for I knew she was in Sarah's mind. Sarah would never forget, and my aunt would be Sarah's yardstick, always, for how a lady should act.

I did not go to look for the sovereigns. Sufficient to know of them. But I too sat silent and thought tenderly of the giver, who this last time had not failed me as she had never failed me. With this money I could take more time to seek a position of work. I could take time to look for a place to live. I would not spend it all. I must leave some of it in case of need, in case I became ill. I am growing up, I thought. Before, I never wondered about the future. Now I am on my own and have no one to help me, I must be sensible, forwardlooking, unprofligate with my money.

Eighteen sovereigns. I could hardly believe it.

Then Sarah began to speak again and what she said had nothing to do with my inheritance. But what she said put all thoughts of it out of my mind. "Your aunt never forbade me speaking of it to you. I've thought about that. I've wondered if I should mention it. I never heard her say, 'You know about this, Sarah. But you are not to tell my niece.' Never once. If she had lived, I would never tell you. It was her business. But now that she is dead, I shall tell. Perhaps, if she had known she was dying, she would have told you."

"Told me what?" I asked.

"You have a sister in London," she said.

Two

I think the recollection of that scene in the parlour will never fade from my mind. I see everything as it was at that moment. Sarah's strong, plain face looking calmly back at me. Of course I do not know how I looked but I remember my pulse raced and my voice was not steady as I said, "A sister? In London?"

Sarah said, as though turning the screw, "A twin sister."

I said idiotically, "Is she like me to look at?"

Sarah said sardonically that since the last time she saw her was when my sister was some six weeks old, she could not tell. "Most babies look alike. You both had reddish hair. You screamed louder."

I have not mentioned the colour of my hair. A shameful red, red as a carrot, an unfashionable hateful colour and something I can do nothing about unless I dye it or wear a wig. I really am ashamed of it. When I was small, I fought the son of the Irish washerwoman here in the village because he shouted. "Fire! Straw on fire!" after me. I knew what he meant and he had hair as red as mine! But I knew that beautiful ladies did not have red hair. They were all yellow as a cornfield or brown or raven black. No gentleman, I sighed, would look twice at me. Fortunately, though, I did not suffer freckles. This would have been intolerable for I saw what they did to the son of the Irish woman. His face was covered with brown spots as if with freckle-fever! But, perhaps to compensate for my hair, my eyes were grey with thick black lashes, my eyebrows black and winged. If it were not for my hair, I thought! I hoped my sister's hair had lightened to red-gold.

My sister. I could not easily take it in. Not to be on my own, after all. To be told the news on this, the darkest day of my life up to now. *I had family.*

The mind-reader who sat opposite me spoke up. "How do you know they want you?"

"Of course they will want me! Who has heard of sisters, meeting for the first time like this, spurning one another? Who took her away? Who adopted her?"

"Your uncle Bigby."

I had not heard of him either. "My mother's brother? Dorcas's brother? Why did she not tell me of him? All these years——" I said angrily.

Sarah interrupted me like a knife flung into wood and stood there quivering, full of menace. "Don't you blame your aunt, not now or ever. It was not her fault. Your uncle wanted just your sister. He did not want you," Sarah said cruelly, "nor anything to do with your aunt. Your mother, God rest her, married a man your uncle said he despised. He told her that if she ran away to marry Bates, she would be dead to him from then on. He told her nothing good could come of it—"

"How do you know all this?" I had to ask.

"I listened at the door," she confessed without a blush. "The day he and your aunt came to fetch the baby."

"An aunt, too!"

"Oh, servant, maid, ox, ass, everything it has in the scriptures," Sarah said. "He came down in great style. He was well off, then. Now he is very rich. A merchant," she said. "In the City of London."

"You did not learn all this by listening at the door."

"No. Your aunt needed someone to talk to. Do you think the less of her for talking to a servant?"

"You are putting words into my mouth," I said, annoyed. I was annoyed because the words were a true description of what I thought.

"Your aunt was a lonely lady."

"Lonely? She had me. She had the school, friends—"

"None of them knew what I knew," Sarah said. "And she could trust me."

Suddenly my anger left me. I stretched my hand across the table and for the moment held hers. I said, "I am glad she had you, Sarah. I know she was fond of you."

A loud sniff was the only indication that I might have touched a tender nerve. I said, "But surely there were people who knew there had been two babies—"

"We lived in Maidstone then," Sarah said. "Your mother is buried there. You know that. And your father. When there was just you, your aunt came here and took all her savings to open the school. She looked after you, and taught in the school. Small wonder she was tired. And the secret. Secrets rest heavy on the gentle of heart," Sarah said. "It is the strong, like me, who can keep secrets best. The kind and the gentle and the sincere are burdened. I do not know if she would ever tell you. I know your uncle ordered her not to, and ordered her to swear it on the Bible but she would not. She said she gave him her word to leave him in peace but she did not believe in using the Good Book as blackmail. Then he left. And we were left with you. There are people," she said, "who would praise him for a generous, good-hearted man to adopt one of the orphaned sisters."

"How do you know he is not generous and good-hearted?" I asked. "You are denigrating him. You do not know him or what he has done."

"I know him by what he has not done. Once, a year or two ago, your aunt wrote to him. She was in bad health. I do not know what she said. But I do know nothing came of her letter."

"How do you know that?"

"Because I read the letter that did come—"

"Sarah—" I said, aghast.

"It was from his place of business, from his chief clerk, to say the letter was received but Mr. Bigby was in no position to reply."

"Well, that is two years ago," I said stoutly. "People change. I shall go to London to see him. When he sees my sister and me together—"

"You should write romances," Sarah said.

I felt a fiery blush come over my cheeks. But I would not lose my temper. I was a young lady now. Life was beginning to unfold before me. Dorcas would understand, I thought, that even if this was the unhappiest day of my life, the day of her funeral, for me it also held the seeds of great happiness, the joy and relief and excitement of knowing I was not alone. I said to Sarah, "You cannot understand. You do not know what it is like to be alone."

"I had seven brothers and sisters," she said. "When my mother died and my father, we were put in the care of the parish, in the workhouse. I went from there to work for your dear aunt. I do not know where one of my brothers and sisters is."

When I could, I said I was sorry. But, God forgive me for an unfeeling girl, I thought it could not be as bad for her as it was for someone with my sensibility. And so much for my thoughts about the iniquities of the social scale! But I said, half to myself, "If I had only known before—"

"What would you have done, miss? Pestered your good aunt, day in and out, to be allowed to see your sister? Sulked until she gave in? She could not be certain they might not break your heart when they refused to see you."

"But I am going *now*."

"*Now* you are on your own. It is nothing to your aunt what happens when you get there, if you get there."

"Wherever Dorcas is, she is looking after me still—" I shouted.

"You would even grudge her a rest from that?" Sarah said, making out that I was selfish.

"Do you not believe she can see us? That she is in heaven, looking down on us?"

She was silent.

I said, "You do believe in heaven, don't you?"

"I have had my fill of it," she said, "in the work-house. We are not talking about heaven but about Lucius Bigby, Esquire, of Mincing Lane in the City of London."

I memorized every word. And she knew I did.

"And if he will go to heaven," Sarah said, "then the rector is wasting his time on Sundays preaching love thy neighbour."

I got away from heaven. I tried another tack. Perhaps I still wanted Dorcas's approval on what I meant to do. I said, "Do you suppose, that if my aunt had—had lived a little longer but known she was to die, she would have told me?" I longed to believe this.

Sarah shrugged. "Only she could answer that. I am telling you all this not to cheer your heart. Not to give you a happy ending to the day. I am telling you what happened so that you will know what a brave woman your aunt was. There is a long word," Sarah said. "I heard her use it and I asked what it meant and I thought it described her. *Indomitable*. That was she. But her young ladies called her Miss Mouse. I told them if I heard them say it again I would clout them, and I would! They said she would not say boo to a goose, and that she was afraid of the wind if it blew too hard. She was the bravest lady I knew, and of a high courage," Sarah said with a simplicity that went to my heart. "She acted for the best when she gave the baby to your uncle. But she must have grieved at the separation. She had promised your mother she would do her best for the babies and this was what she thought best. But it went hard with her, I know it did. It made her feel she had failed."

"Why did my uncle not come to the funeral today?"

"I should have kept my breath to cool my porridge," she said, and I understood, and said, indignantly, "I was listening! You said my aunt was a wonderful little lady and I know it. If I had heard those girls laughing at her, *I* would have clouted them." I corrected myself, "I mean I would have corrected them. But why is my uncle not here today?"

"He does not know of her death. If he did, he would not come."

I breathed hard. "I have told you you are not to speak of him thus. When I know what he plans for me, I will write and tell you and you will feel ashamed."

"Not I. I can tell you now what he will do. He will show you the door."

"When he hears his sister is dead—"

"—He will suffer pangs of remorse and wish he had been a better brother while she lived? He will shower belated love upon you as a sort of atonement?"

"You are enjoying this, Sarah."

"No, miss," she told me. "I am not enjoying it. You are a young, untried, romantic chit who knows nothing of life. We are talking of your aunt who was buried to-day and who was the best mistress a girl could have. I was very young when she took me in. She taught me to read and write, and she said, 'I am your family now, Sarah,' and she meant it. We are talking of a woman with love so deep and so sincere it wore her out. Teaching in the school. Bringing you up. Do you not think, though, that in the nights there must have been times when she worried that she might not have done her best for you? Do you not think that she would compare the riches and the comfort your sister had with what she could give?"

"I would not have wanted to leave her."

"She could never be certain for she set no store upon herself. She used to read aloud. *So he passed over,*" Sarah quoted, *"and all the trumpets sounded for him on the other side."*

I sobbed that my aunt would not care to hear me scolded like this. "I loved her—"

"Then inscribe it on her grave," Sarah said. "A weeping angel to guard the words. No one wept over her when she was alive."

I pulled myself together with some sniffing and wiping of my eyes. I said, "Now you have said what you wanted to say. You have a low opinion of me. But I tell you that I will try to live my life so that Dorcas, if she were alive, would be proud of me."

"Amen," said Sarah, without much conviction. "She used to say she wished she could save you from your loving heart."

"Save me from it?" I said "Did she say that? What did she mean? I should have thought a loving heart the best thing to have."

"She used to say you would go through fire and water for those you loved and not reck the consequences. She said you were stubborn—"

"Yes," I said and nodded and stood up. "But before you make a list of my bad qualities, we will resume the packing and clearing. I am grateful to you, Sarah, for what you did today. Telling me what you have told me. Life is strange—" I said and no doubt would have started upon a dissertation on its strangeness had she not interrupted me with, "One door shuts and another opens—" and picked up the silver tray and went towards the kitchen.

I looked after her and shook my head. I was no match for her. But I promised myself that I would write and tell her how things went when I reached my Uncle Bigby's house. I would describe my welcome, tell her what life had in store for me now, tell her about my uncle and my aunt and my sister. I would not say, "You see how wrong you were in the aspersions, the doubts you cast on these blameless people?" I would not say she should be ashamed. But when she did read of what had happened, she should feel shame.

We worked late to clear up because I was determined to start for London the next day. "You go tomorrow," Sarah said. "I will stay and finish the place. You pack your trunk tonight. Leave the cleaning to me."

Telling myself that indeed she did have a better side to her nature, I complied. I packed my dresses in the trunk and my bonnets in the hat box. Last of all, I sewed the sovereigns into the seam of my dress.

It was from Sarah that I gained the name of a place to spend the night. She said she listened to the talk of my aunt's tea parties when she came in with teapot and hot water jug and plates of cakes. Miss Forfar, a spinster lady whose every action seemed, according to her, the right and proper and indeed the only thing to do, spoke of an hotel she knew which was respectable, comfortable and not too expensive. "Miss Forfar always maintained she felt safe there," Sarah told me. Her tone implied Miss Forfar would have been safe anywhere, being an unprepossessing lady with a loud voice and intolerable manners.

I told Sarah, and I meant it, that I did not know what I should have done without her. Dorcas had left just two very small pieces of jewellery, two brooches. I gave the jet brooch to Sarah. She only nodded and pinned it straightaway to her bosom. I asked if she had chosen where she would go.

"To Miss Farr," she said.

"The General's daughter?" I stared. Miss Farr was a lady who thought herself just one notch beneath Lady Ann. When Miss Farr and her aged father came to morning service on Sunday the swish of her silk crinoline could be heard before she passed you on her way to their private pew. I disliked her intensely. She came to tea with Dorcas because very few ladies asked her to visit, and she spent the time talking about her nieces who went to boarding school and the fees their father paid. It was said she could not keep staff for any length of time. "Will you care for it there?" I asked.

"She has been on to me secretly to leave here and go to her for the last three years," Sarah said. "If she wants me that badly she will put up with my rough ways!"

Then she said, "If things go badly, remember I am your friend."

"Why should they go badly? Even if I did not have my family to go to, I would make a success of my life, Sarah," I said.

She spoiled my dignified attempt to impress by laughing at me.

I went on the carrier's cart to Maidstone. I turned, at the corner of the road, to wave to Sarah but she was not watching. No sentimental farewells for her. I was glad she was not with me because one tear after another fell down my cheeks. I had not known I should cry but the familiar sights of the village where I had lived almost all my life were too much for my composure. It was a bright November day. There had been frost, earlier, but it had cleared to give way to that sparkling air that does come after frost. Cottage gardens were still filled with dahlias and the remnants of flowers. A dog chased a cat over the wall. We passed Miss Farr in her carriage, bent on giving some tradesman in the village a poor half hour. Rooks cawed in the church elms. The spire pointed straight to heaven for those good enough and wise enough to heed its message. I tried not to remember Dorcas buried in the churchyard, her grave raw and new.

And it took so short a time to leave the village. A place which is one's world left for ever by the paces of the horse and some turns of the wheels.

I took the coach to London. When I got there, I took a cab to the hotel. All this, I severely told myself, will stop when I am familiar with the place. I will learn my way here. I will know how to get from A to B, even to Z, on foot. Why did I think this? Why did I bother to consider it? Should I not have thought I would be travelling in my uncle's carriage, after tomorrow?

The sight of the city terrified me. Rain fell now, making sootiness more black. People passed and repassed on the pavements in numbers I would not have believed. I did not know so many people existed in one place at one time. They walked fast, because of the rain, but to me it made them seem more alien, even inimical. They looked so purposeful. They know what street this is, I though despairingly. They are not lost as I should be lost. Sense and reason seemed to recede before such a tide of misery as I had never experienced. I found myself wishing I was back in East Frobisher.

But we reached the place where I was staying and by now I had wiped the tears from my face and tried to take hold of myself and these weak emotions. The street was a quiet one. The place looked respectable. I walked up the steps and entered.

After a meal, I decided I would go straight to bed. I hung up my black dress. I brushed my bonnet where the rainwater had soaked it a little. I wiped my shoes ready for the morning. I dropped my voluminous nightgown over my head, plaited my red hair, then knelt to pray. I did not address the Lord. I spoke aloud to Dorcas. I thanked her for all she had done for me. I told her no real parent could have done more. I would try to be a credit to her. I asked her forgiveness for the many times I must have saddened her.

Then I got into bed and slept. I had thought I would not sleep. But, oblivious of the great strange city outside, I slept like a child.

If my aunt was looking down on me from heaven, she must have thought I was one very small spot in the vastness here, small to the point of being inconspicuous!

Three

In spite of the impression I had given Sarah Prendergast of being stubbornly certain that my family would be on hand to welcome me and to accept me straightaway into the family, I had sense enough to consider they might be away from home when I called. So I had written a short letter, introducing myself, as it were, which, if I could not see my relative face to face, I would present to him by some third person.

The morning was dank and dark. Even as early as this, there seemed to me no freshness at all in the air. Rather it seemed as if it had been used up, all the clean air, a week ago and was now being breathed again and again. Murk was everywhere. It must be difficult, I told myself, to keep up a standard of brightness and cleanliness within the home. Brass would tarnish, curtains get sooty, rugs and carpets muddy with dirty shoes. The pavements were filthy.

Windows had no sparkle. I was reminded for a moment of the sparkling morning when I left East Frobisher. With astonishment I realized this was but yesterday.

I also told them at the hotel that I would like to stay one more night, another piece of caution arising out of the lack of knowledge whether my family was in London or not.

When I gazed from the window of the cab which took me to Mincing Lane, I got the impression that half the population of the country must work here in London! I had never seen such crowds. And the traffic. Drays, carts, barrows. Hansoms and family carriages. Pedestrians crossed the street at their peril but they did cross, darting between the carriages and carts. Costers pushed their wares, boys swept the crossings. It was like a moving picture to me framed in the murk of this dirty November day. I did not see a single smart lady among the pedestrians. But I decided this was not their habitat. This was the place for business men and clerks, messenger boys and all connected with the affairs of business in a great city.

I was very nervous. So much so that I tugged at my right hand glove so hard that the seam split. I could have wept. I only had two pairs of gloves, the other a pair of grey woollen gloves which Sarah had knitted for me and which I had thought not elegant enough for London.

When I reached my destination and stood on the pavement and looked at the sooty building where the sign read *Lucius Bigby, Merchant,* it started to drizzle again. I had no umbrella, and mentally I scolded Sarah Prendergast for not reminding me. You warned me about enough other things, I thought. Nothing as practical as an umbrella.

When I entered, I saw a clerk working on a stool in a room on the right hand side of the hall. I tapped at the window. Irritably he looked at me. I smiled. It made no difference. With what I saw was a sigh of impatience at being interrupted, he came and opened the window. I enquired after Mr Bigby and said I was a relative. This changed his manner. He said he regretted Mr Bigby was not coming into town this week, he had a slight indisposition. He was at his Hampstead home, the address of which he gave me.

Another cab. But this must be the last I take, I told myself. Tonight I shall either be with my family or, if they are not at home, and I have to wait for them at the hotel, I shall learn my way around and walk or take an omnibus.

My uncle's house was impressive if one was looking for size and bulk and not beauty. It was domestic Gothic, red and raw and new. I did not care for it. It lowered, here beneath grey skies. But I thought it might not have glittered over much in summer sun. It gave the impression, though, that its owner was wealthy, and this, in our age, was what mattered. When a man made a fortune, he built a country seat or a town mansion. If he could not exactly show his fellows the extent of his funds, he asked them to visit him!

"*Tradesmen*" the sign curtly said at one side, but I made for the front porch. The butcher's boy went around with his basket to the back of the house, and I was glad to see that the staff here did not live like moles below ground. Not being a mole, I should have hated to spend my working life like this. There were such places all along the road where my hotel was and the sight dismayed me.

I rang the bell.

What truly vexed me was my split glove. What would they think? What would *my family* think? Perhaps they would overlook it but I did not wish to begin our acquaintance in debt to their kindness. First appearances are important. They must not think me slovenly. Dorcas had been for ever preaching that it was the little things that mattered. No holes in one's stockings, no split in one's gloves. I tried to hide the offending hand.

The door was opened by a footman. I had seen footmen before. Lady Ann employed them. This one looked down his nose at me. He wore green livery with a gleaming white shirt. My glove seemed to burn a hole in my hand. He had the sort of eyes that would see that glove, first thing! I enquired after Mr Bigby.

"Charities to the back door," he said.

I bit back a smile. I said, "I have a letter for Mr Bigby. It is not to do with charity. It is for him alone."

He stared at the letter. I said gently, "I think he would wish to see me."

He told me to wait there.

I could not see into the hall for he took the precaution of shutting the front door. A servant who is probably a greater snob than his master, I thought. I stood there and gazed at the garden. Behind the brick wall that separated the house from the road there was grass. No flowers. No trees nor shrubs. Only grass. Now it was sooty and winter-sad. It was not very appealing.

The footman returned and motioned me to follow

him into the house. He gazed hard at my shoes. I would not scrape my shoes on the scraper, not if I died for it, I thought rebelliously. Dorcas would have been saddened by this. I hoped I would not leave muddy marks but I would not scrape my shoes in front of this man. I caught a glimpse of the hall as I hurried after him. He walked fast as though to give me no chance to linger and look about me. Two huge dark chests. The window on the landing was of stained glass. A portrait, an eighteenth-century divine, in oils over the huge fireplace. A suit of armour. Was my uncle collecting ancestors, I wondered, for I was certain our family did not merit a suit of armour.

At a door the footman knocked deferentially. Someone bade him enter. He held the door open for me and I stepped through.

My uncle and I were face to face.

He sat at a desk and all the time I was in the room with him he did not invite me to sit down. The desk was large, leather-topped and imposing. A silver inkwell and a silver pen-stand. A fire burned in the grate and shone on the glass-fronted bookcases. I do not like bookcases. I always think books are happier on shelves where they can so quickly be found and taken down. To me they look imprisoned in a bookcase though I knew the latter were becoming very fashionable now. A painting of my uncle hung over the fireplace in this room. There was a sofa and two armchairs in leather, a globe in one corner and a round table on which stood a green-leaved plant. A stern room.

I dropped him a curtsey. His eyes went immediately, I swear they did, to my split glove. My cheeks flamed. I took off my gloves and held them in my hand. A cold voice, cold as steel, told me not to divest myself of my outer garments since I would not be staying long.

My uncle was small and wizened-looking. His eyes were back in his head. He took off a pair of steel-rimmed spectacles to stare at me. He wore a suit of expensive black wool but I knew he could not be in mourning for his sister.

"What grounds have you for claiming to be my niece?" he asked, and, as he spoke, rolled up my letter and threw it into the flames.

I said, "I am truly your niece, sir. Your sister's child. Your dead sister, Margaret Bates. My aunt Dorcas, your second sister, brought me up."

"And now you have grown expensive and she has turned you out?"

"Dorcas is dead, sir. She died last week."

"So you have come here to seek charity from me?" Not a word about Dorcas.

Was it charity? It must look like that to him but I had not thought it so, up to now. My cheeks burned afresh. I was sure my skirt and jacket steamed in the heat of the room. I wished I might sit down.

"I came because I have no other family."

"Who told you of me?"

I spoke the truth. I said it was the servant. Sarah was able to look after herself, I thought.

"So my fool of a sister is dead—" he said.

"She was not a fool! She was the best and the most generous of women—"

"She was a dangerous, romantic fool. She persuaded your mother to see more of Bates. A weak, vain man. An idiot with money. Did you know your father was a failed music master?"

"I knew his health gave way when he was teaching."

"He would have failed at any job he took! I forbade your mother seeing him but Dorcas connived at it. She helped them run away. I washed my hands of it. But when both were dead, my dear wife, a saint among women, told me it was my duty to take one of the children. Dorcas, she said, will not be able to look after both of them. I do not deny that you are my niece," he said. "You have a sister living beneath this roof, my adored daughter."

When he said this, a transformation occurred. It was as if winter snow thawed and spring sun brought out flowers and blossom. This cold, hateful man smiled when he mentioned my sister, smiled foolishly so that I knew he doted upon her. Then he said, "My wife and I have brought Arabella up to believe she has no family. This is how it will remain. She has inherited none of the taint of her parents but is loving and gentle and amenable in all things. She is the prettiest as well as the happiest girl I know."

He looked at me, looked me up and down and I felt scalded by his look. His face said that he would never consider me anything but a beggar, not fit to be spoken of in the same breath as my sister. I swear that at this moment I felt anger like a red mist before my eyes. They say red-haired people have red-hot tempers. Perhaps it is true because the Irish boy and I had fought like tigers that day. But I took hold of myself. I said, "I came to you with great expectation because I thought I had no family and found I did have an uncle and aunt and sister."

"I admit no responsibility for you," he said. "Your mother was to have married a great friend of mine, a man of means who has since made a fortune for himself in the City. That idiot Dorcas came between my friend and me—"

"Do not dare call her that," I shouted. "So much for friendship if he ceased to be your friend. If someone had come to Dorcas as I have come here—"

"No doubt she would let them batten on her," he agreed. "She wrote me once begging for money. I expect your keep was proving costly. Your sister—" again the smile—"costs me a pretty penny but I do not grudge that. I have more than enough for her pretty whims and fancies. But Dorcas had nothing. I should think that every mouthful you put into your mouth was added up in her mind and she wondered how she would pay that week's bill."

I knew he was deliberately torturing me because this was the sort of man he was. I might be dying within of disappointment and yes, shame after what he had just said about what I had cost Dorcas, but I tried not to show it.

"Yes, she begged from me. I did not give her a penny. I am not a vindictive man," he lied, "but I told her I would never forgive her and I kept my word. No, Martha Bates, I do not want your father's daughter beneath my roof. You will leave now and never return. If you do, the footman will have orders not to admit you. If you persist, I shall find means of keeping you out. I am not without influence. Your sort, spongers and cadgers, are adept at your trade. Give you a shilling and you are back for a pound. A sensitive girl would not have come here but your hide is thick—"

"I will never come again."

"And if I find you have tried to get in touch with

Arabella, who is an angel and you are not fit to breathe the same air, I shall make you sorry for it. I do not wish Bella to know you——"

But here he was unfortunate. At this moment the door opened and a stout lady entered, with much huffing and puffing, followed by a young girl who ran to my uncle, put her arms around his neck, kissed the top of his bald head, and said, "My invitation has come! To the Ball at Raglan House. Tell me I may accept. Tell me I may order a new dress. Tell me Mama may dress up too in all her finery. We will all three go. You know, I have dreamed of being asked to Raglan House. But tell me I may have a new ball dress——"

A look passed between my uncle and the lady I supposed must be my aunt. He nodded and with a shriek she sat down on the sofa. My sister, for it must be she, stared at her. "What is it, Mama? What has come over you?" Then, pointing to me, "Who is this girl? We have told John, times without number, that begging people go to the back door, however deserving the charity——"

"Greetings, sister," I said.

Swift as a snake, my uncle rose, darted round the desk and hit me hard in the face. The blow was painful but I would not cry. I even smiled at him.

"You are an insolent, ill-bred slut——" he stormed. The stout lady moaned an accompaniment. I had a feeling she might be enjoying herself.

I will not say that facing my sister was like facing my image in a mirror. We were alike but it was not obvious because of our difference in dress. I was certain I looked like a bedraggled crow. She wore a striped blue and grey dress with the prettiest silk fringed shawl. Her red-gold hair was dressed in ringlets. But her hair was not as dark as mine. More the colour of nasturtium flowers. Pretty grey eyes when she smiled but now they were slits of suspicion.

"Sister?" she echoed. "What does she mean? I have no sister." Her voice was sharp and high. Here, I thought, I have the better of you. Years of training by Dorcas had given me a low, soft voice. "Nothing is as ugly as a high-pitched voice, my love," she would tell me. "Or a laugh vying with a donkey's bray."

"Who is she?" my sister repeated. "Papa, Mama, tell me who she is for she cannot possibly be my sister. I have no sister." The voice cracked, tears fell. I suspected that with Papa and Mama tears were a frequent weapon. "Is she mad? Is she trying to get money from you? Give her nothing. Get the police, Papa. Tell John to see her off. Why is she here in the study? What right has she to be here?"

"Calm yourself, my love," my uncle begged. "And you, Anselma. Calm yourself."

Arabella's next move was to rush to my aunt's side, to drop to the floor beside her in a sweet flurry of dress, to take hold of the plump hands and hold them tight. A pretty scene. She said, *"I do not wish* for a sister. I have never wanted anyone. I am selfish, I know, but I will not share you two angels with anyone."

I have written it down, word for word, as she said it. It would have done well in the theatre.

They comforted her and I watched. But this was not the theatre. This was life. This was my family, whom I had longed to join and be part of, repudiating me.

"Tell her, Lucius," my aunt said. "Our darling is

brave. She will listen. She might never have had to learn it if this—this trollop had not come here—"

"No, ma'am," I said hardily. "I have not a trade, as yet."

She screamed. My uncle made to hit me again but I dodged the blow.

Dorcas would have fainted with shame.

I listened while my uncle told my sister what had happened, those eighteen years ago, and the tale lost nothing in the telling. I heard that they had made her legally their daughter. He told her that, at first sight, there had been no question which baby they would choose. As if I, the other baby, were akin to a monkey, I thought. "We love you as if you were our own," my uncle said.

"I am your own," she replied. "Your own girl. I cannot share you, the best and dearest of parents. That you chose me is glorious news. Now I know you do indeed love me best from all the world. But send that creature away. She is only here to disrupt and to take what is not hers. She has lived all her life in another place. Now she wants her part of the goodness and richness Papa works so hard for. It is not right. I will not have it. She is not fit to live beneath your roof—" And so on and so on. Tears filled my aunt's eyes and my uncle's. He blew his nose hard.

Arabella rose from the floor and pointed at me. "Give her nothing. You can see what she is by her face and by what she says. Next week she will be back for more."

I told myself that the pain of all this would no doubt come later. The girl really hated me. It was in her flushed face and her eyes. My sister hated me. I did not wish to stay and I said so.

"I am sorry I came. I will never come back. You do not have to fear I will. I was foolish. Living with Dorcas did not prepare me for people such as you. She lived every day by the Golden Rule. She did indeed love others as herself. And I am glad my mother married her music master if your friend is anything like you, sir. You," I told him, "are not fit to live in the same world as people like Dorcas. You are a worm."

"Where will you go?" I heard my aunt ask with some fear. I knew why and I reassured her.

"That is nothing to you. I will get a position and it will be respectable. Do not be afraid we shall ever meet. I would not wish any friends I make to know I am related to you." Then I wished my sister happiness. She clapped her hands over her ears as if I was putting a spell on her. These false kittenish gestures endeared her to her parents. I could see they did. They made her seem still a child. She is no child, I thought. She is hard and self-seeking. She knows what it is she wants and will make certain you give it to her.

My uncle rang for the footman to show me out. "By the servants' quarters, John. See her on to the road and lock the gate. If she ever returns, she is not be admitted on pain of you yourself being dismissed."

When I was outside, I turned towards the Heath. At this moment, I think I craved growing things, grass and trees, not people. I found a bench and, despite the rain, sat there. But I did not weep. Tears would never put out the pain of that scene there in the house. But then, as I had feared, the pain came and I almost gasped aloud at the hurt and terror of it. Like a living cut in my heart, and terror that they so hated me whom they did not know. But the feeling passed. Perhaps I even dimly understood why they had acted as they had done. The had built up a position and nothing must intrude upon it if they did not so wish. Because I was not a stranger, but part of the family, because I had a story to tell which even they must know might not sound all that pleasant to their friends, I was a danger. Time and money and striving had been used to reach where they were. They would defend it at the cost of love and compassion, and think nothing of it.

The had a mansion because they were rich. They were protected from most of life's ills because they were rich. They had rich friends. But to me they did not seem too secure, not if they could be frightened of me.

I would never forgive them, I told myself, but I thought I would forget them. If I were asked if I had family, I would say no and mean it. I repudiated them now. I wanted not to belong to them and to know no more about them.

I thought, Dorcas, my sweet love, what pain he must have given you. I could not grieve for my mother. I had never known her. But Dorcas had given me her whole life as Sarah had said. I will live my life so that you will not be ashamed of me, I thought. And now you are back, Martha Bates, to where you were before Sarah Prendergast told you the news that you thought illumined your life and made the future seem happy and shining. You are alone in the world. The few days when you thought differently are over. Now you face the truth.

I would manage. I would make my way without help

from my uncle or understanding from my sister. Arabella, the social butterfly. Martha, like her Biblical namesake, one of the toilers. No matter. I might, in the end, be as happy as Arabella.

I made my way back to the road. There was a lot to do. I must find a position and find a place to live. I would do it. I felt grown up now in a way that made this morning's Martha seem a silly child. Sarah had known, all along, how it would end. For Sarah knew what sort of man my uncle was. Perhaps I should not have felt it but I rejoiced I had called him a worm. So often, it is after the event we wish we had said such-and-such.

I must look after myself now. This was the refrain which went through my mind. I knew God did not always protect the orphaned child. There were, alas, too many instances when His eyes seemed turned away. Well, one-half of orphaned twins, I thought wryly.

And no more cabs. This time I took a four-horse omnibus.

Four

Back at the hotel I changed out of my wet clothes, shook them and hung them up to dry. The ribbons on my bonnet looked sadly the worse for rain. I changed into my grey dress with the white color, mentally begged Dorcas's understanding for setting aside my mourning attire, put a warm shawl over my shoulders, took up a book and went down to the sitting-room. I was hungry and ate the tea with a good appetite.

But if, here in a different milieu, I had hoped to forget my uncle and his behaviour, I was unlucky because sitting near me was a lady who could have been Uncle Bigby's sister, fitting the role far more competently and sincerely than Dorcas. She sat on a sofa where the wide skirts of her crinoline took up all the space. Seated opposite was the girl she was haranguing, one could not call it "addressing". The lady was very plain, being fat with small eyes embedded in flesh, and a small pouting mouth which she must have been born with and done nothing to cure. Why is it that plain women like to draw attention to themselves? If I were as plain I would dress soberly and behave quietly so that my lack of looks might not be so apparent. Not this lady. Her dress was of rich silk, her bonnet a tall confection of silk and feathers, the streamers tied coquettishly at one side of her dewlaps.

Her voice was as ugly as her looks. I realize I am giving no quarter but remember I had not yet recovered from my visit to Hampstead. I was in no forgiving mood towards the second bully in one day! I held my book in my lap and turned a page from time to time. But I heard every word and very painful they were.

The victim was a girl of my own age, I surmised. She was thin-faced, pale, with the sort of looks I, turnip-Martha, had always wished for. High cheek-bones, an aquiline nose, dark eyes and smooth dark hair in wings each side of her face. She had an air of elegance I longed to emulate. Her hands were slim and white. Here is a lady, I thought. She was not well dressed. Her clothes were old, I could see that. Her shoes were patched. But it was her hat that intrigued me. I had not seen a hat like this before, such smartness had not yet come to East Frobisher. It was round, "porkpie" shaped, in a grey material with a little wing of grey feathers at one side. A hat which gave piquancy to its wearer, a hat, I immediately decided, which made my bonnet seem old-fashioned. I would procure such a hat as soon as possible and wear it as she did, tilted forward. I would wear my hair in two such smooth wings.

I think I have already given some indication that I love bonnets and hats and head-dresses. When I was

small my doll, Clarice, had a collection of hats. Dorcas
encouraged me since she saw that it made me happy
and kept me quiet. Though Dorcas did not know that in
church on Sunday I spent most of the time re-bonnet-
ting the ladies in the pews in front.

But the fat lady in the crinoline evidently disliked
the hat. She remarked upon it. She said, which was a
lie, that it ill became the wearer and she said it was
more respectable to wear a bonnet. Her daughters, I
heard her say, wore bonnets and very sweet and submissive they looked. I thought it a strange word. I had
the feeling that beneath the bonnet brim her daughters,
many times, mught have seemed submissive while in-
wardly seething with revolt.

The girl sat listening, looking down at her hands
clasped in her lap. You, I thought, are the one who
will always be seated at the dinner table next to the ir-
ritating old man with the ear trumpet, or next the curate oo agonizingly shy you rise from the table with a
migraine. You are a martyr to politeness. While I admired her appearance, I wanted to urge her to stand up
for herself. The lady accused her of stubborn neglect of
her relations, and of bringing shame to the memory of
her dead feather and mother. And of her little brother.
How quick they are, I thought, to enrol the dead on
their side. I was certain the little brother did not care.
Then I understood. The lady wished her to go back
with her to Leicestershire to act as governess to her
three younger daughters. "The three older girls do not
need you though you might be useful looking after
their clothes. I cannot understand why governesses
leave us. We give them the standard wage. Not a
penny more for I do not believe in pampering the

lower orders. We feed them and they have a room of their own. They come on holiday to look after the children. I want you to come back with me. We are related. I was your late father, the vicar's, second cousin. Do not defy me. He would not have wished it."

"I am not defying you," said the girl, quietly. "But I am settled here now."

"A milliner. A common milliner," said the lady, spitting out the word as if it was a bad cherry.

I pricked my ears up harder and listened to every word. A milliner. This explained the fashionable hat. "One step removed from a factory worker, for all your airs," the lady squawked. "I cannot tell people, when they enquire what it is you do, for some of them recall your father and ask after you."

"That is kind of them."

"Do not be impertinent. You have an impertinent manner for all that soft air! I command that you return with me. I have it all arranged. Since you are family, I suppose you must eat with us at times. I will give you ten pounds a year. If you say no, I shall not speak to you again. You will be dead to me."

Say no, I begged silently. Save yourself another visit such as this.

The girl said she was sorry but she would not leave her present employment. "I paid a premium to enter Madame Ferrier's establishment. I am an assistant now—"

"You are a foolish ape," the lady shouted. She was, I saw, monumentally disappointed and I feared she might have a stroke on the spot at not bearing this girl back to Leicestershire with her in chains! She struggled up, refused all help with shawl and reticule, and left.

The girl slipped out too but I ran after her and caught up and said, "Will you come back inside for a few minutes?"

"I would not go back there," she said, showing some of the spirit I had wanted her to show, "for any sum of money."

I understood but I said quickly, "I am desperate to speak to you. I need your advice. Is there anywhere we could meet? I am a stranger here. I only arrived yesterday but I would come anywhere to ask what I want to know." I decided to say it there and then. "I want to be a milliner," I said. "I heard you say you are one. It was like a miracle."

She paused for a moment, then smiled and said, "Miracles do happen—"

"In unlikely places," I finished. We looked at one another. She laughed and so did I. I gave her my name. She said her name was Emmeline Fairclough. If I had had time, I would no doubt have sighed with envy of it. *Emmeline Fairclough.* It was as ladylike as her appearance. I said my aunt was dead and that I had no home and had come here to make my living. I think that at this moment she saw how frightened I really was beneath the bravado. Perhaps she remembered what it had been like for her, or perhaps she recalled a time when she had been helped. I do not know. I only know that in a matter of hours from the time my own blood relations repudiated me, I gained a sister in Emmeline.

"I lodge not far from here," she said. "If you come back with me we will talk about it in my room."

The streets were dark now but to me it was spring

and the fields filled with daisies, the sun shining and new lambs bleating. For the first time today I was happy. You are mercurial, I told myself. Perhaps. But better to take the moment and be happy than to dwell on hatred and grief.

She said, "Being a milliner, creating bonnets, is not all sewing pink roses on to silk, choosing streamers. We work hard. When there is a mourning order, I have known us work all night. In the London Season, I think I dream of bonnets—"

"I would work hard," I said. "As hard as anyone."

"I think you would," she agreed. When I asked where she lived, she said in Kensington. "Not the fashionable part, as you will see."

"If the fog ever lifts and daylight comes."

"It is not always November! This is my holiday," she said and when I stared, explained. "We take holidays when there is a slackening of the work. But Madame does look after us well. I am lucky to be there. It is one of the best houses in London. There are thirty girls," she said proudly.

I sent a little prayer up to God that next week there might be thirty-one.

"I board with Mrs Jarrett," she said. "The room is at the top of the house. But the house is clean and Mrs Jarrett is good to me. I have been lucky there."

"Share the room with me," I heard myself say, "and you will halve the rent."

She looked at me. We were beneath a street light so it was easy for her to see the eagerness on my face when I spoke. She smiled, and I believe at that moment adopted me as a younger sister though there was just six months' difference in our ages. Never once, all the time we were together, did we quarrel though there were times when my impetuousness must have tried her. "I know what you wish to say," I went on. "You do not know if Mrs. Jarrett will agree. We will not know if we do not ask her."

"If I can help you, Martha, I will," she said.

Emmeline would have cleared the streets of London of the poor and the sick and the helpless and hungry, if it had lain in her power. She was all goodness. I never knew her to have a mean thought or do a cruel act. I think she loved me. I worshipped her.

When I met Mrs Jarrett, busy, bustling, kind, I exercised all my good manners. We had had a talk in Emmeline's room, then descended to the kitchen where Mrs Jarrett reigned. "Move in tomorrow," she told me. I thanked her with a full heart.

So, next morning, I left the hotel and moved to the Jarrett house. Mrs Jarrett was a widow and gave thanks for being one, she said. Jarrett was dead and she told me that since he had been no good when alive why should she mourn? An honest woman, I thought, though I did not know if Dorcas would agree so I nodded my head. This had been Mrs Jarrett's home when her father was alive, and when he died he left it to her. "He lived with us," she said, "which was a blessing because Jarrett was a big man and I would have had difficulty holding his head under the tap in the yard to sober him up. My father helped me. Jarrett died falling under a brewer's dray. It was the death he would have wanted. Better that than the horrors he was making for."

"Mrs Jarrett," I ventured, "why did you marry him?"

"Bless you," she said, "when it's a bud you don't always see the rose will turn out maggoty." And left me to work this out. I came to the conclusion that Jarrett must have been a handsome youth.

Mrs Jarrett had always taken in lodgers. The farther up the stairs, the cheaper the lodging. First and second flooors were taken by Mr Dee and Mr Diss, city clerks. Mr Dee was chief clerk in some business, so he had the first floor. Mrs Jarrett served them as if they were blood royal, and, being canny men, they knew how lucky they were and, though the address was unfashionable, they would never move. When we met, I murmured a greeting, cast down my eyes, dropped a curtsey. Gravely they raised their tall black hats.

Mrs Jarrett told me, early on, I would be good for Miss Fairclough. Like cough mixture, I thought. She said Miss Fairclough was a lady, a perfect lodger, but sometimes seemed too quiet to fight life's battle. "Now you," she told me, "can give her gumption." I said I would do my best. She was a dear, good woman and Dorcas would have liked her. She did us all sorts of kindnesses and we paid our rent regularly every Sunday.

We slept, Emmeline and I, in the same bed. Beside the bed was a table with a box-like space beneath for the usual bedroom receptacle. Ours was white with blue flowers, pretty save that it had no handle. I told Emmeline it was pretty enough to grow flowers in, and she blushed when I said it.

On top of the table was a bowl and pitcher. We fetched water from the tap in the yard, a long walk down the stairs but we were young and strong. The drugget gave out on the stairs after Mr Diss's room but we didn't mind. Also in the room was another table where we ate, two chairs, a little rug Mrs Jarrett gave us. We boiled a kettle in the grate and sometimes made toast there and cooked what we fancied. Usually we went down to the kitchen to cook or brought food home from the market.

When I moved in there was just one chair, of course, so the first thing I did was go to the second-hand stall in the market and haggle with the man there for a chair. I found I had a fancy for this though Emmeline did not find it easy. And I think the stall-holder fancied me for he ogled and winked through he was a villainous-looking man with grey stubble and ratty hair. But I smiled at him and got the chair for a shilling. I gave two street urchins two pence to carry it back to my lodgings. "Find out where she lives," the man told them. "Tell him Windsor Castle," I told the street arabs. The said they would but only for another penny.

Mrs Jarrett and I washed the chair thoroughly. She gave me a cushion for it. She also gave me a jam jar to keep flowers in. Mr Dee and Mr Diss gave us a bunch of flowers as a moving-in gift to me. I was very pleased. "In spring," Mr Dee told me, "there are flower sellers at the corner near the church. I think you will patronize them." When I asked why he thought this, "I never saw a girl who betrayed her origins as you do," he said. "A country girl. Those pink cheeks—"

"I wish to look a Londoner as soon as possible," I sighed.

"Pale cheeks and a tired tread?" he said. "Always in a hurry? A frown between the eyes which is part smart-

ing from fog, part peering to dodge the oncoming
crowd—"

Was this how he saw his Londoners? I said, "Where
do you come from, Mr Diss?"

"North London," he said. "But it does not mean I
approve. It is a terrible city. To live here is an imposi-
tion. As if one has been condemned to it by some
celestial decree—"

I had to say it. "Then why do you stay?"

He told me it became a habit.

I still hoped I would soon look like a Londoner, by
which I meant someone as slim and as elegant and as
quietly certain of herself as my friend Emmeline.

Within a week she had introduced me to the owner
of the establishment where she worked. When she went
back on Monday she had mentioned to Madame's second-in-command, Miss Moses, that there was a young
lady who would like very much to be taken on. "We
have two vacancies," Emmeline told me, that evening.
"Two girls have left. You may be lucky, Martha."

I nodded, almost sick with excitement. To steady my
nerves I asked Emmeline if I might borrow her best
pair of gloves for the interview.

Five

My respect for Madame Ferrier was sometimes close to fear for she could be intimidating, cold as ice. To look at, she was tall and personable, with black hair and dark eyes. She was a very successful business woman. If there were times when I wondered if she did not have her accent on a leash, by which I meant she had not been born to those cultivated tones but acquired them, no matter. Her establishment was one of the best in London, favoured by the rich and the well-born. Her bonnets were very expensive.

She looked after us well. Compared with some conditions with some milliners, Madame was revolutionary. She believed she got the best from us if we were well in health, and content. She paid us well, fed us well, gave us holidays when times were slack. Her workrooms were airy and light so that we did not strain our eyes, particularly sewing jet on black. (How

I hated mourning orders! And there were so many of them.) We even had a sitting-room for our use. If we were ill, a doctor was sent for. The hours were long, true, but we knew Madame cared for us, and we responded.

Of course we gossiped about her for very little was known of her private life. Some said the old man who cleaned up the steps and looked after the "area" was Mr Ferrier. Some said Madame had been the mistress of a Duke when she herself was a poor milliner earning nine shillings a week. Some said it was the Duke who gave her money, at the instigation of his new Duchess, to start up on her own and be independent of his Grace. The Duchess would stand a mistress but not a mistress who was a milliner.

I thought I would not wish my husband to have a mistress. I would want to be the world to him so that he would not look elsewhere. But then, I should not marry. I was determined on this. Families are not necessarily a good thing, I told myself. Think of Uncle Bigby. My family had died for me with Dorcas, and she was exceptional. So, no family for me.

But one thing the heartbreak with Uncle Bigby did, and this was to harden my nature. Now I truly believed I was nearer Sarah Prendergast and her cynicism than to Dorcas and her love for others. I knew well now that life is a battle.

But I tried to be friendly at work. I liked most of the girls and I think they liked me. Some were rough and some gentle.

But to describe my first meeting with Madame. She interviewed me in a small workroom which was empty at this time. It might have looked bleak to someone else with its uncurtained windows, its bare scrubbed floor, table and benches and chairs. To me it was the Promised Land.

When I told her I was an orphan, she told me that sometimes she felt if she took on another fatherless and motherless girl she would be entitled to write *Orphanage* above the door. I told her I did not think I could afford a premium. I had to earn my living.

She said, "You must prove yourself before I think of admitting you. I have my own way of doing this. I neither know nor care if it is unique but I find it useful to separate the girls who are enthusiastic only about being a milliner from those with a flair for it. Because a girl likes trimming bonnets, it does not mean she can create what I am looking for."

She told me I was to stay here on my own and materials would be brought to me. I was to create a bonnet for a young lady of eighteen years. "Her first Season. Young, pretty and rich," she told me. I nodded. I think I looked round-eyed as any owl but she left me there and soon I was brought boxes of silks and ribbons and velvet and flowers and lace.

My eyes must have gleamed when I saw all these enchanting materials and trimmings. There was silk as blue as a summer sky. Forget-me-nots like those that grew near the stream that ran through East Frobisher where I had lived. I used to bring bunches of the pretty flowers back to Dorcas with cowslips and marsh marigolds which she would put into a jar and put this on her table in the schoolroom. For the moment a mist blurred my eyes, thinking of those young and carefree days. I made myself think only of my work, my test.

I imagined a fair-haired little beauty, indulged and

spoiled by loving parents, dancing through her first Season, wearing such a bonnet to complement her white swaying crinoline at a garden party, a blue parasol, blue mittens and little blue slippers. Blue and white as the sky above her. I worked all morning and well into the afternoon. I made a bonnet of blue silk with blue silk streamers, lace edging the brim and beneath the brim forget-me-nots so tightly packed you might think that if you pushed a finger into them—as I hoped you would not—you might feel the soft sweet moss of a river bank.

Then a thin severe lady entered, picked up the bonnet, examined it minutely. And sniffed. I was disappointed, mortified. I came to know that Miss Moses had a scale of sniffs for bonnets. A confection beautiful enough to make the angels envious, tulle and roses and lace, merited a delicate sniff. A bonnet not up to her exacting standards brought a sniff so fierce it was a wonder she did not choke on it. When I was a permanent member of the staff I came somewhere halfway up the scale of sniffs. Miss Moses, the second-in-command, the All-Seeing, the Law-Giver. I once heard Miss Moses and Madame burst into laughter together, and I have seldom been so astonished.

She went out and I stayed there, praying for success. She returned to tell me Madame would take me on. I thanked her. She sniffed. Then she told me the rules of the establishment, my rate of pay and so on. "Madame says that since you missed your midday meal, there is a meal for you in the kitchen." There was. A splendid meal of meat and potatoes and a vegetable. A pudding with currants. I think I ate like a she-wolf. But with manners.

I asked if I might wait for Miss Fairclough so that we might return together. She told me I might go into the workroom and start working. Then she said, "Take note of Emmeline Fairclough. She can teach you much." This made good sense to me and I promised that I would.

The establishment was in Hanover Square, and in the mornings Emmeline and I were two in the flood of girls and women making for this area. We dressed as smartly as we could. When we disappeared into the dressmakers' houses, and the milliners', it was to work to make others stylish and smart, and we worked hard at it. We envied our sisters who went decked out to parties. Of course we did. But I think most of us were happy.

I know I was. I enjoyed being what I described to myself as lapped by beauty. I loved the look and feel of silk and velvet and lace and ribbon. I could smile over the perfection of a silk rose or a cotton daisy even. I would smooth the streamers when I had finished the bonnet, and pleasure in it.

"Martha Bates—sniff!—you are dreaming. Get on —sniff! with your work."

Of course I had never in my life seen such bonnets as were created here. *Bonnets in the French Style* the gilt letters read on the discreet board that swung on its iron arm at the front of the red brick house. Paris was a magic word for fashion. *The French Style* captured imagination and purse, and well Madame knew it.

"You do not make bonnets," Miss Moses told us. "You create them." And so was born in us a pride in our achievement.

Every bonnet was original. No bonnet was copied.

We worked in straw, silk, gauze, lace and velvet. For trimming, ribbons, pearls, jet, braid, feathers, flowers and fruit. Yes, cherries and berries. But always, Miss Moses's voice rang out. "Remember, nothing bizarre. Our taste is impeccable." It was the motto of the establishment. Hats were gaining in popularity, especially among the younger women, but the bonnet still reigned as favourite. After all, there was the example of the Court.

I longed for Madame Ferrier to be able to add By Appointment. I had visions of her walking up the steps of Windsor Castle with Miss Moses and some of the girls behind, each with a hatbox. Alas, by the end of 1861, Victoria and frivolous bonnets were parted for ever, and life was one long mourning order—for the Prince Consort.

I discovered, early on, that I particularly liked creating bonnets for young ladies. Give me a scattering of daisies, cornflowers, the blossom of cherry or apple, straw pale as wheat and ribbons blue as a summer sky, and I could have a bonnet which put you in mind of picnics and parasols and open-air parties, perambulators in the Park, *fête champêtre*. When I had almost finished it, I silently addressed my unknown client. "Wear it and look your prettiest. Captivate some admirer. For when you are married, such bonnets will not become you. They will be for your younger sister." Thinking this, I usually tucked in another rosebud.

Madame once told me to remember there were other ladies beside young ladies. "It is the middle-aged and the old with the lined faces who pay for bonnets such as you make for their young daughters. The mothers deserve a little of your genius too."

I knew the word was offered with sarcasm but I always tried to do what she suggested or ordered because I was so very grateful for the chance she had given me. So I did try to create bonnets for what I called older ladies of thirty.

I became, inevitably, too clever for my own good. I got into serious trouble by making for myself an exact replica of a bonnet I had made for a young Marchioness to wear on her honeymoon in the Italian Alps. It was, I thought, the prettiest, the most charming I had ever made. I could hardly bear to see it packed ready to be sent round to Grosvenor Square. I had made it in different shades of stiff blue ribbon, one shade merging and melting into the next. It would, I told myself, look perfect with her red hair. I craved that bonnet. This had never happened to me before. I think Martha Bates, the person, peeped out for once from Martha Bates, bonnetmaker.

The Marchioness, I knew, was the same age as I was. So I copied the bonnet at home with cheaper materials. No one would know, I told myself. The Marquis and his bride would be abroad. But there was an unwritten rule in the workshop—unwritten because Madame would never have believed a girl would do this—that no bonnet was to be copied. Emmeline tried to talk me out of it but I was stubborn. I made the bonnet. Mrs Jarrett said it was a beauty. I wore it out of the doors twice before one of the girls saw me in it and reported me to Miss Moses. I never knew who the girl was. One does not strike up an acquaintance with worms.

Madame, when she interviewed me, told me to my face I was a thief. The Marchioness had paid for the exclusive use of the bonnet. "I should have thought your sense of ethics would tell you this," she said. I did not know what ethics were except that I obviously did not possess them.

I stood in front of her desk. The carpet was soft beneath my feet. It was a pretty room. Rosewood furniture, pearl coloured hangings, a silver framed mirror. A peacock feather fan in the grate. To me it might have been the Old Bailey.

"Your trouble," I heard her say, "is that you do not recognize what your place is. You are not a law unto yourself. You work for me and you are a milliner. *What are you?*" she demanded.

If I died for it, if she dismissed me on the spot, I could not have said other than what I heard myself say. The words issued from my lips and I could not stop them. I said in a whisper, "I am Martha Bates, ma'am."

We looked at each other. The only sound was the ticking of the little French clock on the mantelpiece. She said, half to herself, "What will you do, where will you go if I dismiss you?"

But I was not going to play upon sympathy. I said, "I deserve to be dismissed. I will try to find another job."

But she said she would not dismiss me. She said she believed I had learned a lesson. She said that if Martha Bates, individual, was so important to me, I was to make sure I was proud of the name and did nothing to demean it. "Or you will get into trouble," she said. "One cannot go through life considering oneself alone."

I wondered momentarily that if I did not consider

Martha Bates, who would? Well, Emmeline would. But I must not be a burden upon Emmeline. I said heroically I would get rid of the bonnet.

"Yes," she said. "You will burn it here in my grate." I did and she watched me and I shed a few tears over it.

But from that day on I was reformed. I kept in check any excesses I felt might overcome me so that I forget my lowly status and in the opinion of some think myself the equal in rank of those above me. Excesses I would indulge in after working hours. This did not give me much time, but there were days, when work was slack, when we finished earlier, and on these nights Emmeline and I often went to the theatre.

Oh, not to the Haymarket or Drury Lane but to a rough little theatre in Eel Pie Street. Mackays, it was called. I had never in my life seen a stage play and I was enthralled with every act and word. Indeed, when we were turned out into the street after the performance, I was for a long time still with the play and the players, reliving it. I tried to go as often as I could and Emmeline accompanied me. This did surprise me because I would have thought that with her clerical background she would not approve of the stage. The ladylike Emmeline did not hiss the villain nor shout and cry as I did but she enjoyed it and contented herself with clapping when virtue, as always, was rewarded, and villainy got what Mrs Jarrett called its "come-uppance."

It was at Mackays we met Jamie.

Jamie Moore. He was an orphan too, and worked at the theatre. His parents were actors and when his mother died soon after his father old Ma Mackay let

Jamie stay on. He was odd-job boy about the place. Sometimes he acted a small part though he was a shockingly bad actor. Usually he saw to effects. "*Make the cannon roar, Jamie,*" we would shout. Sometimes we shouted to wake him up because he had not come in on cue. His mind was somewhere else, not on tonight's blood-and-thunder! But everyone liked him, laughed at him and took it as part of Mackays. Jamie was thirteen. A thin, gangling fair-haired boy, with honest blue eyes and a sweet mouth. He had told me he did not wish to be an actor. "Just as well," I said. Then he confessed that he wished to write plays. I did not reply to this because I could not see how it would come about since he was getting no education. Jamie could read, and did read voraciously, but I did not know if what he read stayed in his mind for he read to escape from life.

When I say that everyone liked Jamie, Quentin Diamond detested him. I do not know if this was Quentin's right name. Perhaps not. He was a walking bag of conceit. I think he was a relation of old Ma Mackay for she doted on him but I did not think he would be a rod and a staff to her in her old age for Quentin, I was certain, had fixed his sights on the fashionable theatres across the river. If they beckoned, he would be off. Meanwhile, he grabbed all the death-or-glory parts here at Mackays. We put up with him because the play had to have a hero but we preferred old Mrs Howard, fat and corsetless, who was the hero's mother or the villain's weeping grandmother, smiling through it all. Or Joe Spence who drunkenly forgot his lines and was cued by us in the audience when Joe would hold up the action on the stage, advance unsteadily towards the footlights, bow to us and say in his beautiful voice coarsened by drink, "Thank you. I needed that."

Quentin never dried up and if he had, we would have let him be prompted by someone else. I was sure that one day Quentin would sack Jamie for he truly hated him. I do not know why except that perhaps Jamie's basic sweetness of nature was proof against Quentin's bullying. Try as he might, Quentin could never get Jamie to weep.

Jamie lodged in Cupp Court where he paid two shillings a week for his room and bought his own food. Mrs Jarrett was good to him because, when she used to "go to the play," as she called it, she said she had been in love with his handsome father. Whatever the reason, she saw Jamie did not starve. He was growing like a bean and always hungry.

Jamie treated Emmeline with respect but she confessed to me she did wish she might get him to laugh with her as he did with me. I think I looked upon him as a younger brother. When he talked to me about writing plays but confessed he wished he had an education, I thought of the books Sarah Prendergast was storing for me. I asked Mrs Jarrett if I might store boxes in the cellar and told her why. When she said yes, I wrote to Sarah. A short letter. She would understand what had happened with Uncle Bigby by my address, the news I gave of my position, and what I did not say. The letter came promptly in reply. *Thanks for yours. Glad to hear you have settled down. Job here fair. Money good. I have prospects. Respectfully. S. Prendergast.*

I could not think what prospects these might be and decided I must write, some time, and enquire. When the boxes of books arrived, Jamie looked as if he were in heaven. The books were not in the boxes more than a week. Jamie borrowed them and so did Mr Dee and Mr Diss. But I made certain Jamie had first pick and when he could not understand a word, I explained. Sometimes, he and Emmeline and I read Shakespeare together, each taking parts. Mrs Jarrett said it was a fair treat to listen to us.

In my conceit, I came to think I had "adopted" both Emmeline and Jamie. Perhaps I had forgotten the first day when I threw myself upon Emmeline's kindness and begged her help. Now, happy and working hard, I took her under my wing, it seemed to me. I looked after her, saw she was warmly dressed, ate her meals, did not do someone else's work as she might easily do through kindness of heart. I had made Jamie happy, I thought, and conceit swelled within me. Was it conceit? Or was I still trying to assuage the terrible hurt I had suffered that first day here in London? Did I want to prove that people liked me and came to me and chose me as a friend? Perhaps this was so. When I faced the truth I believed I might never, whatever I pretended, recover from that interview with my uncle.

Once, I saw my sister and my aunt in Regent Street. They were stepping from their carriage, bowed into a perfumery shop by a lackey. My aunt as fat as I remembered her, Arabella in pink with bonnet to match and parasol. I loved Regent Street. When I had a message to take to one of the stores, I would try to get it over quickly so that I might linger to look in at the windows. I could never afford to buy the French gloves, the Indian shawls, the lace and the ribbons. There were hosiers and stay-makers, haberdashers and mantle and gown shops. It was Aladdin's cave to me.

But this day, when I saw my sister and my aunt, I felt for a moment as if I had turned to stone. But, recovering, I fled from the place. Then I knew, sadly, they still had power to make me feel a nothing person, one they wished dead. Emmeline, that evening, asked me what ailed me. Something did, she said, for I was not in my usual spirits. I told her nothing had upset me, and would she not pester. If I lost *you*, I thought, I would indeed be lost and have cause to feel myself dead.

"You have a loving heart, Martha," I heard her say.

I told her Dorcas had said this of me, so I had been told.

"It is true. I think you would go through fire and water for your friends."

"For my friends, yes," I said.

She reminded me of the poem by the seventeenth century poet Herrick. *"To Anthea Who May Command Him In Anything."*

When I started to speak, she held up her hand and smiled and said she knew the poem was that of a gentleman addressing his lady. "But I apply the words to you, Martha." And she quoted them to me in her sweet voice. *"Or bid me love, and I will give A loving heart to thee."* And at the end, *"Thou art my life, my love, my heart. The very eyes of me. And hast command of every part, To live and die for thee."*

"You do me too much honour," I told her.

"I do not. Where you love, you give your heart. When you marry, he will be a fortunate man."

"I shall not marry. But you," I said, turning the conversation away from me because, if I did not, I should weep at what she had said, "you will marry a curate. And have a quiverful of children."

"Martha!"

"Psalm one hundred and twenty-seven. *'Lo, children and the fruit of the womb.'* And two verses on. *'Happy is the man that hath his quiver full of them: they shall not be ashamed when they speak with their enemies in the gate.'* "

She looked at me. I stared back. Perhaps, since we were quoting the psalms, we should not have dissolved into mirth but we did. "Yes," I said, "there is a curate somewhere who does not know what a pearl among women he is due for. You will marry him, and I—"

"Yes, Martha? And you?"

"I will buy up Madame's business," I said. "Descend upon you in your country cot and take your oldest girl back to London with me—in memory of the two of us here now."

So passed for me one year and three months in London. I had survived as a bonnet-maker the hectic London Season, four fashionable marriages and I do not know how many mourning orders. I had seen spring come to London when the teasing March wind tugged my porkpie hat off my head and sent the fringed ends of my shawl around my face. I had walked in the Park with Emmeline beneath a brilliant summer sky. The fogs of winter had depressed me for the second time. Oh, I was a Londoner now. Like many or all from the provinces, I had adopted the great city with the fervour of a convert.

Then came a day in February 1862 when it might be true to say the second part of my life began. What had happened up to now seemed preparation.

Six

Miss Moses told me to take two bonnets to an address in Mount Street. I was delighted with the outing. Mount Street was not far away but I would take my time. When I arrived at the house I did not make the mistake, as at Hampstead, of knocking at the front door. I went down the steps and to the servants' entrance. But, strangely, when I told them my errand, I was taken into the morning-room and told by the footman to wait here.

Alone in this elegant room, I laid the boxes on the floor and stared around me, frankly inquisitive. The floor was carpeted in blue and the hangings were of the same shade in velvet. Velvet over net. I sat on an upholstered chair and arranged my skirt around my ankles. I sat very straight. I think the quiet room made an impression upon me. There were framed water colours on the wall which was papered in a pretty striped cream and blue. There were pictures in silver frames on the mantelpiece above the grate in which a bright fire glowed. I sighed for the comfort of wealth as much as for its elegance.

I glanced over my shoulder. The door was firmly shut. I unbuttoned my boots, slid my feet out of them and tip-toed over to the fire, holding my feet up to the blaze. Right foot, left foot. What bliss. I returned to the table. Emmeline would be ashamed of me.

Did I say my chair was next to a round table covered wih a chenille cloth? On it stood a silver dish, tall with a stem and a solid base. I think its name is a tazza. It was filled with a mouth-watering collection of bon-bons and sweets. Barley sugar, crystallized violets and rose leaves, marzipan in different colours and shapes. Studiously I tried to look away. It was no use. My eyes returned to the dish and its contents. Some of the sweets were wrapped in gold foil, some in striped waxed paper. They looked expensive. Probably French, I thought largely, as if I daily bought a pound of such sweetmeats in a shop in Regent Street. How pretty the little sugar plums were, frosted and silvery.

The first sweet I ate was marzipan. I was very hungry. I had had little breakfast, being late for it. I had eaten an apple on the way to work but this was all. If the sweets had been especially concocted by Satan for my downfall, I could not have fallen more swiftly. They were delicious but lasted so short a time. I nibbled at a rose leaf and a violet petal. I could not decide which I preferred.

The decision was made for me. A large masculine hand reached over my shoulder and pulled the dish closer towards me. "Take your fill," a voice said. To me it might have been Jehovah!

I swallowed what was in my mouth, fortunately not choking on it. I rose and turned to the newcomer. I realized I did not have my boots on. Desperately I felt for them on the carpet. "Take your time," the same voice told me.

I found my boots and put them on and buttoned them. Then, red-faced but not wholly from bending to button my boots, I faced him at last.

He was tall and good-looking. Black hair and grey eyes. Not an old man. Older than I was, though. He only looked at me now, saying nothing. Before my inward gaze marched a series of events perhaps ending in prison. Was stealing sweets as bad as stealing bread? Worse, I thought. Stealing bread meant you starved for food. Bon bons are flippant. Did they still transport people to Australia for this crime? I heard myself say faintly, "I do not think I should fancy Australia."

"Then why go?"

"For stealing."

"They ceased that practice, for poaching at any rate, four years ago."

"Thank God," I muttered. And I said that if I were dismissed from my employment, I did not know what would become of me.

"Do not blackmail me," he said and emptied the dish on to his spotless clean handkerchief, then offered it to me. I recoiled as at a snake.

"Take them," he said.

"No, thank you, sir. I should not have fallen a prey to temptation—"

"Are you always so prosy?" he asked.

"No," I admitted. "Only under stress, I think."

He turned a laugh into a cough. He said, "You are Martha Bates? Madame said she would send you round with the bonnets." He smiled at me but I did not smile back. I was frightened to death. Madame Ferrier had warned me, before. Here I was now up to my neck in crime. What would Emmeline say? Would she want to share bed and board with a known thief?

I said, "In some far off lands I believe they cut off the right hand of a thief."

"I think they did it here once," he said, "so it has nothing to do with geography."

I did think he had a good voice. Low and amused, cultured. Please stay amused, I silently begged, then I may get off with only a warning, not a report to Madame.

Then I said, "Sir, I have come to deliver two bonnets to the lady of the house. I would be glad to do so. Perhaps there may be some alteration she fancies—"

"I ordered the bonnets," he said.

Of course. For his mistress. I tried to look worldly wise. I wondered what it was like to be a mistress.

"Show them to me," he said, indicating the boxes. I bent to put them on to the table but he was quicker than I. He put them there himself. I smiled at him. He stared at me and said, "You are a dazzler when you smile."

I had no answer to this. I dared not frown, I was too much in his debt. I could not say thank you. That was not my place. I said, "These are my bonnets. That is to say, I created them."

"I know you did. Madame Ferrier told me. That is how I knew your name."

When I had opened the pretty striped boxes, I took out the bonnets and showed them to him and I must have smiled as proudly and as foolishly as a mother with her pretty baby. They really were delicious. One was of yellow chip straw, more than a hint of the country belle in the wreath of daisies and buttercups, the streamers like good thick country cream. The other was lilac with lilac ribbons and a froth of lilac blossom beneath the brim.

"I do prefer to design for very young ladies," I admitted. "Madame tells me not to forget older ladies of thirty, though."

He coughed. But he said, "And do you wear these frivolous delights yourself?"

"No, sir."

He looked at me. "There is a story here and one you are not going to tell me. I shall ask Madame—"

"I would rather she was not reminded," I said.

"What did you do? Copy a bonnet you made for some rich, mindless chit and wear it on your elegant and beautiful red hair?" he said.

He was teasing me. My hair was my worst offending attribute, as I have said. To be beautiful and elegant you must be red-gold like my sister and have a rich Papa to indulge you. I heard him say swiftly, "I am sorry. I did not mean to tease. I meant it. Your hair is beautiful."

"Sir," I said, "about the sweets—"

"Damn the sweets—" he roared. "Forget about it. Of course I shall not tell Madame. How can you think it? Now come upstairs."

I took a deep breath. I had been in London long enough to know of its dangers, its pitfalls for the working girl. If you desired to remain chaste, you must be constantly on your guard. In the workroom, I had heard tales that figuratively set my hair on end. Of girls accepting invitations and never being seen again. One of the girls with us was called One-Slip Meg for the burden of her stories. "One slip, and you are ruined for ever."

I put the bonnets back into the boxes and slowly re-tied the ribbons. Then I faced him. I hope I looked haughtily cold. Like Lady Blanche in *"A Woman Scorned"*.

"Do you go to the theatre?" he said.

"Yes."

"Drury Lane? The Haymarket?"

"Mackays," I said. "In Eel Pie Street."

"What the devil are we standing for?" he said. "Sit down." He indicated the sofa, waited until gingerly I sat, and sat opposite me. He crossed his long legs and smiled. I sat stiff backed and unsmiling. I glanced be-hind me to see how far away the door was. He said, "Tell me about Mackays."

I told him a little. I spoke of Jamie. I said I went with my friend Miss Fairclough but the words came out stilted. I was unhappy and I was afraid. He sighed at last. I believed I knew what he was trying to do, try-ing to make me feel at home so that I would give no thought, in the end, to what I hazily called my honour.

"Will you bring the bonnets upstairs?" he said again, and I said, "No, sir."

It is one miserable thing after another, I thought. I was found out copying the bonnet. I steal sweets here in this house. Perhaps he will tell Madame I have been rude to him. I felt the tears rise.

"For God's sake," he said wearily and no doubt he was within his rights to feel so, "I have no designs upon you. Do you think Madame Ferrier would send you here if I had a reputation for—for—"

You may well choke on the word, I thought, censorious now. But when I peeped at him, he was laughing.

"I will ask one last time," he said. "Will you bring the bonnets upstairs and display them?"

"Not if two housemaids carrying a bonnet box apiece went ahead and behind me," I said. I rose, pulled my shawl tightly round me, picked up my gloves and reticule. I said, "I am only a milliner and you are a gentleman of means—"

"Set that to music and the Halls would love it! Very well. Good day, Miss Bates." He rang the bell. A footman appeared. "The young lady is leaving," he said.

For one wild moment I was seized with a desire to say I had changed my mind and would go upstairs with the bonnets. Was this, then, all my honour meant? That when it came to leaving this charming stranger, and he was the best-looking and most charming man I had ever met, I was prepared to accede to his request for some further time with him? Dorcas, I silently implored, wherever you are, stiffen my resolve!

In the street, I passed through the crowds without seeing them. I believed I had fallen in love. And I did not know his name.

Seven

Next day I was recalled to Mount Street.

When Miss Moses told me at work that Madame wished to see me in her room, I thought, *"He has told on me, after all. She knows about the sweets."* And my heart was filled with disappointment because I had thought him a gentleman to keep his word.

He had kept his word. Madame Ferrier knew nothing about my misdeeds. If she had, she would have done more than mention it when she had me standing before her. She told me I had to go back because of the bonnets. I put one construction on this, that the client found something wrong with them. Rebelliously, I thought, "How dare she? They are perfect." Martha Bates, thief of sweetmeats, might be glad to be reprieved but Martha Bates, milliner, was upset at what must be criticism. I nodded stiffly. Madame looked down at the top of her desk. Then I said craftily, "Before I go there, Madame, may I know the name of our client?" Perhaps thus I would learn his name.

"The bonnets are for Miss Bertha Hatton," she said. I thanked her while thinking this was not what I wished to know.

When I arrived, the footman led me up the stairs, and knocked at a door. A voice said, "Enter." He announced me as "The girl from Madame Ferrier's, Miss Hatton."

The girl from the bonnet shop, I thought.

It was a very pretty room, a bedroom which also served as a sitting-room. A tester bed with rose striped silk hangings. Chairs and sofa upholstered in rose silk. Flowers everywhere. Vases of daffodils and bowls of hyacinth and crocus. Spring was here in the room. Great vases of leaves bursting into green, packed hard into the vases. And books. Books spilled over on to the table and chair and bookcases. But these bookcases were my favourite, open shelved. Over the mantelpiece a portrait in oils of a little girl in mob cap and white dress, blue sashed, with two spaniel dogs. Silently I marvelled, as I had yesterday in this house, at the comfort of it all.

And my tall, dark gentleman was here. I saw this, first thing. I dropped him a curtsey.

He smiled, the warm smile I had remembered, all last evening. "Miss Bates," he said, in acknowledgement. "I did not introduce myself, yesterday. Robert Hatton."

"Sir—" I murmured and curtseyed again.

"It is a polite gel," a voice drawled from the bed. "Come here, child, where I can see you."

I was used to such voices. We thought them aristo-
cratic, in the workroom. A voice which called a girl a
"gel." "The gel who made my bonnet." And I am
afraid we mimicked them.

The coverlet on the bed was of rose silk, the sheets,
I saw almost disbelievingly, of silk. Imagine being
lapped in silk when one was asleep and not aware of it!
Propped against a pile of pillows was a tiny middle-
aged lady. I saw she was tiny because she lay outside
the bed clothes. She was no taller than a twelve-year-
old, I thought. She wore a silk dressing-gown patterned
with flowers and—I stared—on her head was my lilac
bonnet. The face beneath the bonnet was thin, pale,
with a long nose and small eyes. In my nervousness I
could see long white whiskers transforming the little
face into a kind-looking Mrs Mouse! She did look like
a mouse. I bade myself frantically to stop such
thoughts. I think it was the sight of my bonnet above a
face which was, to put it kindly, years too old for it.

"Do not be nervous," she said. "We are harmless."

"Well, comparatively," said the well-remembered
voice from behind me.

"You thought your beautiful bonnets were for a chit
of seventeen," said Miss Hatton complacently. "They
are for me."

"She did not think that," the voice said. "She
thought something very different. And she thought they
were, in their way, cheese for the mouse—"

When he said mouse, on top of what I had thought,
when he reminded me of how ridiculous I must have
seemed yesterday, the shaming tears fell down my
cheeks. If I could have worked out revenge, it could
not have been better. He swore at himself. I heard. He

swore at himself for being an insensitive boor. Miss Hatton bade me sit down. I did in a silk-covered chair. I hoped I would not slide off it. She rang for chocolate and biscuits.

"These gels—" she said, "work so hard. They don't eat enough."

"Oh, no, ma'am," I said, taking hold of myself. "Ours is the best establishment in town. Madame gives us good meals and looks after us well."

"She is a good creature," she agreed absently. "Then why are you weeping?"

I tried to explain. "I was foolish, yesterday. Being foolish in company, being proved foolish, makes me weep."

"Robert was amused," she agreed. "But then he was angry."

I apologized.

"Not angry with you," she said. "He has a tender heart, my nephew—"

"Aunt Bertha—" he interrupted. I could imagine how he felt. She was a tiny lady but nothing and no one would stop her saying what she wished to say. "He could never shoot pigeons," she said.

"And how is that for a recommendation?" he asked. I could see, and delighted in it, there was splendid *rapport* between aunt and nephew. They were genuinely fond of one another.

The footman brought in a tray with chocolate and cups and a plate of Savoy biscuits. Ladies' fingers, my favourite. They were delicious and the chocolate hot and sweet. They each ate two biscuits, I think to keep me company, and Miss Hatton urged me to sweep the plate clean, as she said.

"The bonnets were a present for me from Robert," she told me. "It is not my birthday. No anniversary. But the sun was shining and he said the flower sellers had bunches of snowdrops. He bought me snowdrops and ordered two bonnets. I told him to tell Madame Ferrier I wanted something to remind me of warmer days. I wanted the youngest and the prettiest she had to offer. And I have them—" she said, smiling at me.

"Oh, ma'am—" I said delightedly and could say no more.

But I was very angry with myself for what had happened yesterday, my foolish fears and my pride.

"I cannot walk far," she told me. "I suffered a riding accident when I was young. So I sit here, with a bonnet on my head, to make believe, perhaps, that I am young again and in the Park and the sun is shining—"

"You are playing for sympathy," he said. "You know you never indulge in make-believe. My aunt," he told me, "is one of the happiest, busiest women I know. She wears a bonnet in bed because it makes her brain work harder."

"True," she admitted. I was lost in this exchange between them but delighted in it. She seemed as young as he was. She said, "I have a bearer, and he is genuinely this, called Solomon Figg. Is not that a lovely name?"

Worthy of Mackays, I thought, and nodded.

"Solomon carries me round like a child," she said. "He drives my carriage when we go down to the country. I usually ask him his opinion of my latest bonnet. I think he is waiting for me to wear a confection that beats Nature. Perhaps yours will do this." Then she said, "I wear a bonnet in bed because I am a writer."

I could not, hard as I tried, see the connection but owlishly I nodded.

"There is no connection," she said airily. "I feel the bonnet sets the scene, that is all."

"The scene?" I repeated, nodding. I heard a laugh behind me and wished crossly he would sit where I could see him. As if he understood my thoughts, he moved and sat lounging on the window seat.

"Do you know your fairy tales?" she asked me.

"*Cinderella?*" I ventured. "*The Sleeping Beauty.*"

"I rewrite the story," she said, "from an unpopular viewpoint. The Frenchman Perrault first published them over one hundred and fifty years ago. *Cinderella. Sleeping Beauty. Red Riding Hood. Hop o' my Thumb.* And so on. I am writing them, as I say, from another viewpoint. For instance, I am rewriting *Cinderella* describing the life she gave those two sisters, a whining, miserable creature who could not even make her own way to the Ball. And I describe the state she left the castle in. *The Sleeping Beauty.* What if, when she woke up, she did not like what she saw?"

I had never considered this.

"Look at her face—" Miss Hatton commanded. "She is thunder-struck—"

"I am not surprised," he said. "Compared with what she does, I believe she is wondering how anyone could consider what you do a life's work."

My protestations were cut short when she said, "If I did not occupy myself with my beloved fairy stories I know what I should become. Money mad. I should read nothing but balance sheets, profits, ventures, partnerships. I am," she told me, "immensely rich. It is like a dragon breathing at my back. I come from a family which cannot help but make money. Both sides," she said chattily. "Everything they touch turns to gold. Midas would have envied them. So I read nothing but fairy tales."

I breathed hard. Tonight, perhaps talking this over with Emmeline, I might come to some conclusion. At this moment I had myself to take a tight grip on reality or I too would be in the realm of fairy tales.

"Ma'am," I said, "will you please tell me in what way you wish the bonnets altered?"

She stared at me. "Why should I want them altered?"

"Because Miss Bates, from experience, believes that when she is summoned back to a house, it is to alter her handiwork to the whim of its wearer," he said.

"Pass me the mirror," she commanded. I jumped up and passed her the mirror from the dressing-table. It was very pretty, the dressing-table. White wood with gilt roses and cherubs round the mirror. I caught sight of my face in it. My eyes were bright and my cheeks pink. If it were not for my awful red hair, I might be passable.

She looked at herself in the mirror. "No. Nothing is to be altered. You think it is too young?" she asked me. "Of course it is. But then, the difference is so great between my face and your bonnet, it is piquant rather than ridiculous."

"*It is merry*," I said, speaking my thoughts aloud. "It is a happy thought. And please, ma'am, you will never be old."

"Bravo," he said.

I told her I would be delighted to make her bonnets, if she wished.

"That is what I am coming to," she told me. "I asked you here because I wish to buy you."

The silence fell deep as night. My fears swept back. Had they got me here to lull me with chocolate and Savoy biscuits only to abduct me?

"Miss Bates is fearful again," Mr Hatton said.

"Of what?" she said, perplexed.

"Of us. She thinks we are ready to—to—" He grinned and looked at me. He said, "What would they say at Mackays?"

I would not reply. She took pity on me. "I only mean, child, I want to employ you. Robert's mother, my sister-in-law, has her own dressmaker. My own mamma had three seamstresses in the country. They did not sew for anyone else. I want your exclusive services. I will pay you well. I have some sixty bonnets—I am not exaggerating—and am always adding to them. They are my family. I never, alas for my meanness, give one away. With some, it is lap-dogs. With me, bonnets."

Like Ulysses with Circe, I must stop my ears, I thought. How I would enjoy serving her! She was eccentric, yes, but she was kind, one could see she was. There would be opportunity, too, if I was in her employ to see her nephew, sometimes. Surely?

I told her I was fully aware of the compliment she paid me but I had to refuse. "I have dependants, ma'am."

"Family, you mean?"

At the word, my face changed. I felt that it did. I knew my voice, when I spoke, would be changed too. It would be hard and cold. The word had power to do this. I said, "Not family, ma'am. I have no family."

"What then?"

"I have, so to speak, adopted a pair."

"A pair of what?"

"Friends," I said. I told her about Emmeline and Jamie.

"You snuggle together like birds for comfort?" she said.

"Something like that, ma'am. So you see, I would not wish to leave them."

"I wish I had a pair of heads," she said, "and might offer your friend employment too. Though I would not know what to do about the boy. Tell me about him."

I did. Then Mr Hatton said, "And what is your ambition, Miss Bates?"

"To get Emmeline married to a curate," I said. "To help Jamie, but I do not know how, to become a playwright. For myself, I would like to own an establishment like Madame Ferrier."

"You will marry," Miss Hatton said

"No, ma'am," I replied. "I shall never marry."

They looked at me. I stared at the fireplace. I heard Miss Hatton say, "If you were free of Miss Fairclough and the boy, would you consider yourself then? I mean, only consider yourself and your own plans?"

"I should find someone else," I said. "I am that sort of person. I feel sometimes I am carrying an invisible umbrella and inviting others to shelter beneath it. Perhaps," I said, "because for the first few days I was in London I had no umbrella and it rained incessantly and I have come to look upon umbrellas as not only necessary but a great comfort." But remembering the first two days reminded me of Hampstead and I rose and begged to leave. She said goodbye. So did he. The footman escorted me to the front door and also bade me goodbye in a friendly manner. I imagined it was a good house to work in, with just and kind employers.

When I returned to Hanover Square, Madame sent for me. Of course she knew why Miss Hatton had wanted me, and now wished to know what answer I gave. She nodded when I told her. I was under no illusions that she might say, "Thank you, Martha. I do not know what we should do without you." Something made me say, "Madame Ferrier, I beg you to forgive my curiosity because that is what it is, but I have been to the house two days running. They have been kind to me. They seem kind and interesting people—" I stopped, I heard myself floundering in circles.

Strangely, Madame did not rebuke me for enquiring. She said she would tell me something about the Hatton family on condition I did not repeat it nor gossip in the workroom. But first she said, "Martha, you have no foolish romantic thoughts in your head about Mr Hatton? I know what girls are like. I should. I have employed enough of them to know what silly creatures they can prove. Mr Hatton is indeed a kind young man. Personable and charming, a rich bachelor—"

"Oh, ma'am," I said and tried to sound horrified, tried to widen my eyes that they appear candid and honest. "You mean, a girl might fall in love with Mr Hatton at first sight? As they do in novels? Not for me," I said. "I will never fall in love." And lied, saying it.

"I knew we should not escape histrionics," she said. I did not know what these were but listened while she told me something of the family in Mount Street. This house was but one of their homes, used when they were in London and for the Season. There was a vast estate in the country near the coast, one in Scotland, one in Yorkshire, and a castle in Spain. "Mrs Hatton's fortune is derived from iron works and coal mines," said Madame. "She is the second Mrs Hatton. Miss Hatton, whom you met, has a fortune from the Caribbean. Sugar, I think. I have heard it said," Madame pondered, "that money makes money—"

I thought of my uncle Bigby.

"'With the Hattons, it is true," she went on. "Though it has not brought complete happiness. Miss Hatton, as you perceived, is an invalid. But a rare bright spirit, an example to all of us." Madame smiled so fondly, I was surprised. "The first Mrs Hatton died when Robert Hatton was born. There were two brothers and a sister by the second wife. Both boys are dead, alas. The sister, Miss Rose Henriette, is a spirited, handsome girl. I expect you will see her here when she calls. She is bound to marry well."

"So Mr Hatton has only his father?"

"Yes. And the gentleman never leaves the north country. He is one," she said, "who has so great an admiration for the Middle Ages, or the romantic conception of that time, I am certain he is vexed he was born when he was! However, he has the money to indulge in dreams. He is never happier than when he has organized a tournament or a jousting in the grounds of the Castle. Perhaps his favourite reading is the Poet Laureate's *Idylls of the King*," she said. I was astonished. I did not know how she knew all this. "About looking after his enormous heritage," she said, "I do not think it overmuch concerns him. His son is conscientious to a degree. He works hard. Mr Robert loves the land. He spends a lot of time in the north. I do not think he likes London, though." There was silence. I knew she had not stopped thinking of all this and I wished she would think aloud. But she said briskly, coming disappointingly back to the present, "Are you satisfied, Martha Bates?"

I was not. I wished to know more, to know everything she could tell me about him. I wanted to know if he was not lonely, with an eccentric jousting father, born into the wrong century, a step-mother and step-sister only. I would like to know why he was still unmarried for I knew enough about London society to know he was, as the vulgar mamas would say, "a catch." I wanted to know where this country home was so that, who knows, one day I might go down and look at it. I wanted to know so many things. "Thank you, ma'am," I said and left.

That night, I told Emmeline Miss Hatton had wanted to discuss the colour of the ribbons on the lilac bonnet. A white lie but I was not going to tell her of my offer. I did describe Miss Hatton and the room and said a little about the nephew. We sighed, lying side by side in our bed, for silken sheets. But she did not know that when she was asleep at my side, breathing deeply and peacefully, I felt the cold tears on my face for thinking back on to the day and not thinking in any way about Miss Hatton, dear and amusing and kind as she had been, but remembering every look and everything he said, and his laugh which lit the grey eyes and made his face younger. Romantic notions? Do not entertain them? They engulfed me.

Please God, I prayed, let him find a pretty loving wife. He has so much wealth, she will surely not need to be rich. So let him take time and find his heart's desire. Let them have a strong loving family. And please, dear Lord, lessen the feelings that plague me and give me back soon my old good sense.

The next week we went to Mackays theatre. It was a military play. Quentin was a captain, Jamie a private. There were brigands and Quentin looked heroic in a blood-stained bandage when he rescued the heroine. And it was a night when Jamie's thoughts were elsewhere. This was plain. Twice, Quentin yelled, "Men, where are you?" before Jamie hurried on, buttoning his red tunic as he came, only to collide with the soldier coming from the other side of the stage, and they both fell on the floor. Quentin waited until the laughter stopped. "But one day," I told myself, "Jamie's absent-mindedness will make Quentin dismiss him."

Then Jamie forgot the effects. I myself shouted, *"Make the cannon roar, Jamie—"*

Quentin said, leaning tiredly but with grace against a cardboard rock, "At last, a peaceful spot—" when bang! went Jamie with the cannon. As farce, it was perfect. We laughed like a pack of lions roaring.

The chief brigand—old Joe Spence, drunk as a lord—had to be cued by us and said, "Thank you. I needed that."

By now, our gallant hero was so angry he fluffed his own lines. An impartial audience might have felt for him on so awful a night. We, who heard tales of Quentin's attitude towards the others, were not impartial. We knew how cruelly he treated them, from Joe Spence to Jamie, and we were glad he was getting something back. Even the sympathetic Emmeline laughed at him.

Quentin was helped by no one. We whistled. He turned his best side to us, his best profile. We knew he thought it his best. The other players told us. He stared into the wings. I suppose he was calling for the prompter. A wonder he could have heard a prompter in this din.

Then, in a lull in the whistling and laughter, a voice shouted clearly, *"Come on. What have you got there? A mirror?"*

I turned to stone for a moment. I knew that voice. I looked round. Three rows away was Robert Hatton.

Eight

I was quiet for the rest of the play, my mind in a turmoil. So quiet that Emmeline asked me if I felt ill. I said no. When we got outside there was no sign of Mr Hatton and I was glad. I felt overwhelmed with shame that he had seen me half rise in my seat and shout to the players. Still, it was done now. There was nothing I could do about it. I suppose he had come to Mackay's out of curiosity to see what one of those theatres was like.

On our way home Emmeline sighed that she did not suppose Jamie would be at the theatre for much longer. Not even a day longer. Quentin Diamond dismissed him that very night. We only heard this two days later. We were very busy in the workrooms and I must confess that the face that came into my mind as I sewed and stitched was not Jamie's.

But I did go round, at last, to Cupps Court to look

for him, to be told he had left. On the way home, with Jamie the centre of my fears now, I thought, thank God, he is too old to go up any chimney. I was afraid he would go to sea and be shipwrecked and eaten by cannibals!

But the next night he knocked at Mrs Jarrett's back door. We were all three in the kitchen, she and Emmeline and I, and when I saw him I hugged and kissed him in relief. In classic manner he had his few belongings tied up in a red handkerchief. He looked hungry, dirty, alone and friendless. He said he had come to give me back a book of mine he still had, and to say goodbye. He said he could not stay in London on his own. He was afraid if he did it would devour him.

You *will* write plays, I thought. You have the feel for words.

Devour him. It might happen. The great dirty sprawling, unfeeling, uncaring city might devour him, greedy as it was for the lives of the helpless and the destitute, the homeless and the weak. No room here, I thought, except for the predators. The cunning and the bold, the shrewd and the moneymakers. The rest are indeed devoured and cast out. No hope for Jamie, young, gentle, half-educated, trained for nothing. I bit my knuckles to stem the tears.

It was Mrs Jarrett who came to our rescue. And with her action my thoughts, so black and fearful the minute before, lightened and receded to the back of my mind. There were the evil ones, and there was Mrs Jarrett. For my uncle Bigby there was Robert Hatton. Perhaps, I thought, when a sparrow falls, it does not indeed go unnoticed!

For it is when I feel helpless against great odds to

aid those I love that I feel low. I am one who, if I were a man, would want to be St George, on a golden day, riding full tilt to kill the dragon. Nothing less for me. Mrs Jarrett was one of the vast army of practical women who are aware what a great help a full stomach is. "Here's a bowl of soup," she told Jamie and sat him at the table and set before him a steaming bowl of meat and vegetables. A crust of fresh bread. She tied a towel round his neck for napkin. She ordered him first to say grace for his meal. He did. He thanked God for his good food, amen.

While he ate his soup, and I had never before seen spoon travel to mouth so fast, I found my face wet with tears. "It's you," Mrs Jarrett told him. "You worry her. She has a soft heart."

Yes, I thought, and an untrained mind to go with it. It is I who think I have adopted you and Emmeline and will guard you and look after you, come between you and trouble. But it is Emmeline who is calm. It is I who have broken down. I am not strong, after all. I am the fearful one, thinking cannibals might eat you, thinking you might die of hunger here. Then the thought of Jamie serving as a meal for cannibals or alternatively dying of hunger himself made me choke. "Hysterics, now," Mrs Jarrett said, disapprovingly.

Jamie said, "It was when someone shouted to Quentin about a mirror. And you all laughed. I've never seen him so angry. So he sacked me." The blue eyes, troubled at one moment, glazed over and, if Mrs Jarrett had not swiftly moved the soup bowl, now empty, Jamie's face would have fallen there. He was asleep.

Mrs Jarrett had to be told about the mirror and laughed so hard she said she would crack her stays.

Then she said Jamie could sleep here in the kitchen tonight. Tomorrow, Mrs Jarrett would get him a job as carrier-out with Spilkin, the corner grocer. Spilkin had a great turnover of boys who left to better themselves as grocers' assistants in the stores. "Then he can do some scrubbing of my steps," said the good woman. "He'll feel then he isn't here on charity."

"You will surely be rewarded in heaven," I said.

She said never mind the reward. What she was looking forward to was a good rest and no sign of Jarrett. Bitter as the night was, she shook Jamie awake, then she and Emmeline took him to the pump in the yard and washed him while I washed the crockery. Mrs Jarrett gave him a clean sack to dry himself with, then slipped over his head a nightshirt of the dead Jarrett's. Jamie slept on the couch in the kitchen, with the mice and possibly cockroaches for company. To him, it must have been bliss.

Spilkin took him on. "A good boy but a dreamer," was the verdict. "He will never make a grocer. Not sharp enough. But the motherly ladies like him."

Would Jamie ever make a playwright? I wondered.

February gave way to March. The Season started in April in London. In the workrooms we drowned in bonnets. But I heard a little about the Hattons from a Yorkshire girl who came to us. She was living now with her grandmother in London but she knew the estate of the Hatton family. She said Mr Hatton had what she called a "great do" once every year. Everything was a replica of what a tournament must have been like in the days of King Arthur. And when the day's jousts were at an end—and there was a pavilion built for the ladies, she told me, with pennants flying, only the ladies were dressed in today's clothes, not wimples and so on—there were huge banquets. "Ee," she said. "I've heard the ale flows." She said Mrs Hatton, wimple or not, never attended. "I don't think she cares much for Yorkshire," Katie said, astonished. "Though she comes sometimes. But she travels on the Continent. Like a queen, Mrs Hatton. Cold and proud. I think she wants Miss Rose Henriette to marry royalty and sit on a throne. Then there is the mad auntie who can't walk."

I was ready to defend the "mad auntie" whose passion for bonnets paid some of our wages when Miss Moses entered. I swear she could smell gossip in the workroom from fifty paces! She separated Katie and me.

I dreamed that night—one thing Katie told me that Mrs Hatton never travelled with less than fifty trunks and cases—that fifty-one such pieces were travelling from Yorkshire to Mount Street. In the fifty-first I was snugly ensconced, in some miraculous way not suffocating! When we reached London, I jumped out to be told by Robert Hatton I was not needed and was to go home to East Frobisher.

One morning in late March Madame bade me once more to deliver bonnets to Mount Street. I was delighted. "For Miss Hatton, Ma'am?" I enquired.

Not this time, I was told. They were at the request of Miss Rose Henriette Hatton.

So the family were here in London? For the Season, I supposed, and I wondered if Mr Hatton was here too and if I might catch a glimpse of him. I knew, had been told, that he did not care for London but surely, my soaring spirits thought, he will be there to escort his sister and mother. So filled was I with surmise and conjecture, that when I reached the house I forgot "my place" which it seemed I was only too prone to do. Ask my uncle Bigby! I used the front door instead of taking the bonnet boxes to the servants' entrance.

After I rang the bell I remembered where I should be but by now it was too late.

The footman opened the door. I smiled and greeted him. In the hall were two young ladies. One was fair and pretty but spoiling her looks at the moment by scowling with bad temper. "Fair sizzling" as we said in the workroom. She had hair the colour of primroses, it was so fair. The corners of her mouth turned down. Her silk dress was of violet colour with a bonnet to match, and a parasol of the same silk. You will feel the March wind very keenly, I thought, until I saw a second footman with a beautiful Indian shawl over one arm.

The second young lady was my sister. She was dressed in pink. They made a pretty pair, like fondants. Arabella's face did not change when she saw me. I expect she thought that one day we were bound to meet again. She did not look as cross as her companion. She looked cold as ice.

A French governess completed the trio. She was dressed in black with a *chic*, a smartness that I knew could only be French. When Miss Rose Henriette berated me, the Frenchwoman only listened, not remonstrating, as if it was no business of hers.

"What do you want?" Miss Hatton demanded of me.

I apologized. I said I knew I should have gone to the servants' entrance. "I can only say my thoughts were elsewhere—"

"Do not believe a word," my sister said and her voice was as hard as her looks. "One knows this type. A girl who dislikes people like us, who will do all she can to pretend she is our equal. A pity," my sister said, "she does not darn her gloves. Shoes and gloves," she told me, "are the hallmark of a lady. It does not matter which door you enter."

I did not glance her way. Mutely I offered the boxes to the footman.

"Oh, no," said Miss Hatton. "No, indeed. It is not his place to accept boxes at the front door. We have a boy in the basement for that. You go there and hand them to him. But first, you will apologize for appearing here."

"I have already said I am sorry."

Her voice rose. "Then say it again. I shall complain of your impudence to your employer, if not."

I said I was sorry. "Well, go on—" she said as I turned and poked me in the back with the tip of her parasol. I heard their laughter as I went down the steps. "Does that make you feel better, my love?" my sister asked.

"Lord, how I hate these uppish chits of milliners," Miss Hatton agreed.

Next day, Madame Ferrier told me I was to return to Mount Street. I said, very politely, I could not do so. She looked at me. "Madame," I went on, "if you dismiss me, I cannot go back there. I used the wrong door—"

"I have had a complaint from Miss Hatton," she said. "It arrived yesterday afternoon. Of course you did wrong. Why will you not keep your mind on your work, Martha? It leads you into trouble."

Were we to be just mechanical people, I asked myself. A girl walking in a London street with a gay March wind in her face, flower sellers with daffodils and violets, the sun warm with the promise of spring, silly romantic notions flooding into her mind because she is twenty years of age and thinks she has fallen in love. Nothing can ever come of the loving but it fills her mind. Love brings such hope, hope in minute shape like pretty mice scurrying in and out of the wainscot. A hope that I might glimpse him, at any rate hear his name mentioned, at least tread the stairs where he trod, enter his aunt's room. Then I remembered, the bonnets had not been for his aunt but for his sister. Well, he might have entered where she was trying them on.

"Martha—"

With a start I came back to where I was.

"I am warning you not to daydream and you do it in front of me—" But she sounded more weary than annoyed.

I said I was sorry. I thought if I had a golden sovereign for every time I had to say I was sorry, I should be a rich girl within six months.

"Dreams do not come by indulging in them," Madame said, "but by hard work and application. What happened yesterday?"

I told her. I told her I had angered Miss Rose Henriette Hatton. I told her she had poked me with the parasol. Why should I not admit it, I asked myself, but I was not prepared for the wave of anger that came over Madame's face. For a moment, she could not speak. At last she said, "I do not usually treat lightly my girls who issue me with edicts such as 'I am not going to that house again.' But in this case, send Emmeline Fairclough to me. It is not young Miss Hatton who asks for you today," she said, "but her stepbrother."

I am of all females damned, I thought, as I left the room.

But I could not be jealous for long of Emmeline. I thought he, and perhaps his aunt if it was in her room they met, would be enchanted with Emmeline. Who could not be? Not jealous, no. But this was the first time I had walked home alone from work, and loneliness enveloped me like a fog.

When I reached the house it was to be told that Jamie had left. "In a carriage, like a lord," said Mrs Jarrett. "The coachman brought a note from Miss Fairclough to put my mind at rest that the boy was not being abducted. When I went down to Spilkin, 'Look out for a new carrier boy,' I said. 'For this one's hour has come, that I know.' Miss Fairclough said all will be revealed when she comes home tonight."

I understood Miss Fairclough had not couched her message in these words but in her early days Mrs Jarrett had been a great playgoer too, and had remembered the lines. It was nearly nine o'clock when Emmeline returned, in the carriage. She was brimming with news.

She said Jamie was studying at Mount Street. "Here is the rest of this week's wages, Mrs Jarrett, for you to give to the grocer. It is by Mr Hatton's request."

She has said his name, I thought. Did he ask after me?

"Mr Hatton was sorry not to see you, my love," Emmeline told me. "I could not explain your absence. I said that perhaps you had a special order to finish."

"I would not go there," I said. "I went yesterday, and had a disagreeable experience."

"But they are so kind—"

"With the step-sister."

"She was not there. She is in Hampstead with a friend. But there was a friend of Mr Hatton's there," Emmeline said and blushed faintly. I looked at her but almost determinedly she went on. "You know, Mrs Jarrett, Miss Bertha's bedroom is a salon too where she receives her family and friends. We had a meal there, she and I."

"What did you have?" asked Mrs Jarrett, immediately.

"A light meal but delicious," Emmeline said. "A spinach soup. Roast fowl. And almond pudding. Miss Bertha—she asked me to call her this—has the appetite of a bird but I did justice to it. And a great peach, afterwards." Her dark eyes grew larger as she remembered the peach.

"They eat light, the gentry," Mrs Jarrett agreed, "when they don't eat hearty." And after this piece of wisdom which I could not follow, she said, "What about Jamie?"

"Mr Hatton's friend is a clergyman," Emmeline said.

"Ho-ho," I said myself. "Now we are coming to the cause of the blush on your face."

"Martha, I beg you not to be facetious," she said but the smile on her face put dancing dimples into both cheeks. "The Reverend Julian Emmett."

Emmeline Emmett. I tried the name in my mind. It was not as good as Emmeline Fairclough.

"Martha—" I heard her say— "I know what you are thinking, and you are to stop."

"Never mind her," Mrs Jarrett said. "Go on about Jamie."

"And go on about the curate," I added.

"If you will not interrupt—" Emmeline told me. I promised I would not.

"He is staying at the Hatton home in the country, recuperating after a serious illness. He and Mr Hatton were at Oxford together and are very good friends. When you spoke about Jamie, Mr Hatton became interested, Martha. He came to Mackays to see Jamie. Did you see him there?"

"No," I said, asking forgiveness for the lie.

"He said Jamie would not make an actor. I said we thought this but hoped one day he might get the chance to write. I told him how good you were to get your books sent here and how avidly Jamie read them. But I said he had had small education. I said we loved him for his sweetness and honesty. I said Quentin had made his life a misery in the theatre because someone as vain as Quentin Diamond could make no impression on Jamie."

I could see her saying it, and imagine what an impression it had made on the young curate. I said, before I could stop myself, "Is the curate married?"

"No," Emmeline said before she could stop herself. "I said the good Mrs Jarrett had got Jamie a position with Spilkin after Quentin dismissed him—"

"Not a position," Mrs Jarrett said regretfully. "A carrier-out. A position is behind the counter with the cheese-cutter."

"Then Mr Hatton said, 'What about it, Julian?'

and Mr Emmett said, 'I shall enjoy it, and think it a privilege to carry on where the young ladies and Mrs Jarrett left off.' "

"He said that?" Mrs Jarrett echoed. Then, "Ma Mackay has been good to the boy too. Be fair."

"I said she had given him a job," Emmeline admitted. "I said it was difficult not to like and be concerned about Jamie, and that it showed a vain, mean nature to dislike him. So Jamie is to live in the country with Mr Emmett at the Hatton house, and Mr Emmett will tutor him, and eventually they hope Jamie will go to Oxford. All their reward, they said, will be a ticket for the first night of Jamie's first play. And not," said Emmeline, "at Mackays with Quentin as hero."

We hugged each other with joy, she and I. Jamie we really did love as a brother and were delighted at what had happened. Mrs Jarrett brought out some wine and said I must make a toast to Jamie. "You are the girl for words, Martha."

Let Emmeline be in the company of the curate, I thought, and she does not lack words either.

I thought hard. They must be the right words and from the heart. Then I said quietly, raising my glass, meaning every word: *"Make the cannon roar, Jamie."*

Emmeline and Mrs Jarrett said it after me, the latter wiping her eyes.

Jamie would make the cannon roar, one day, in his own play, in his own behalf, if this was what he wished for. We had no doubt of it.

Nine

Jamie's goodbye letter to Emmeline and me was blotched where his tears fell upon the page. He said he would write often, when he was grown up and earning money he would keep us both, and Mrs Jarrett too if she needed it. If we were in trouble, we were to write to him.

Emmeline looked very tired by the end of the summer, paler than usual, listless. I heard her toss and sigh at my side in bed in the long hot nights. I would be glad when the time came for her to have a holiday, and I hoped passionately we might share the same weeks.

I told Jamie, in a letter, about Emmeline. He told Mr Emmett who discussed it with Miss Bertha Hatton. The upshot of all this passing on of information was that Miss Hatton said we were to spend a holiday in the country. She would pay our lodgings and fares.

Did I say the names of the villages near the Hatton

home were Great and Lesser Ezekiel? The Hatton mansion was just called the Big House but the names of the villages enchanted me. I said so to Jamie in a letter and, of course, he told his mentor, Mr Emmett, and in the next letter he quoted Mr Emmett as saying the English had "great felicity" in such things. Jamie told us "the nobs", a description he did not get from Mr Emmett, lived in Great Zeke, and the tradesmen and work people in Lesser. Of course, I thought. *The rich man in his castle, the poor man at his gate,* and thought there was a sad strain of cynicism in me. Jamie described the houses in Great Zeke as being filled with retired admirals and generals and people who had lived in India for some time. I could imagine their ladies.

"We shall see the country at its loveliest," Emmeline dreamed aloud. "Red-gold leaves falling, crisp mornings, gardens filled with purple daisies—"

"What if we go in January?" I asked.

"Build a snowman," Mrs Jarrett said. "Put a hat on his head, call it Jarrett, then knock its head off for me!"

But perhaps Madame and Miss Moses had noticed Emmeline's tired looks and she and I were given the last week in October and the first in November.

I wondered how I could smarten Emmeline up for the holiday. She always looked elegant but nevertheless there was a shabbiness about her clothes. We could seldom afford new clothes, and going to and from work each day was hard on them. I told myself she was bound to meet Mr Emmett and must look her best. Mrs Jarrett came to the rescue. She opened up a black trunk in which were stored suits of her father's and Jarrett, and two pretty gowns, one blue, one brown. "I was thin once," she said briskly. "No use railing against the fat now. I like my food so there it is!" She held the gowns against Emmeline. "New lace at the neck. Invest in a dozen pearl buttons—" and brushed aside Emmeline's thanks. She surprised me, in my delight at Emmeline's good fortune, when she said, "I am sorry I have none to fit you, Martha." I had not considered it. It was Emmeline I wanted to deck out. I said I had my grey dress I had when I came up from the country. "Perhaps I will buy lace and buttons too."

Secretly and quickly, in our room, Emmeline and I made a new bonnet for Mrs Jarrett. A rich-looking black velvet with black feathers and black satin streamers. "Oh, classy. Stylish," she said as she tried it on. She laughed at herself in the mirror, tucking in some gray hair which strayed, coquettishly turning from one side to the other. "This will knock them when I wear it to chapel."

I had to say I did not know she went to chapel.

"I will in this," she said.

But I was not to accompany Emmeline in my shabby clothes, after all. The day before we were to leave, Madame summoned me. I expected to be read a lecture on how to behave, how to conduct myself if we were to meet our benefactress. In short, how not to bring disgrace on Madame Ferrier.

She came soon to the point, saying she did not suppose I had new clothes for the holiday. I said no, but that I did not mind since Emmeline had been fortunate. She said Emmeline had told her of Mrs Jarrett's kindness.

Then she said, "You will find that the world is divided into good people and bad. At times, it may not appear to be so. The cruel and the thoughtless appear in the ascendant. But there are many like Mrs Jarrett in all walks of life. They cannot help but be shining good any more than they can help breathing." Then she told me she had a friend of the same height and size as myself. "She too is a generous woman. I asked her if she had a gown she has tired of, and explained about you going on holiday." She pointed to a box in one corner. "There is a gown for you, Martha, also a cloak. After your trip to the country, they will see you through the winter in town."

The cloak and the gown were both green, trimmed with braid. I suppose I looked like a Christmas child, speechless with delight at such an unexpected gift. When I could speak, I thanked her for her thoughtfulness, and asked if I might have her permission to write to her friend, thanking her. "No need for that," she said. "Now send Miss Moses in to me."

Emmeline was as pleased as I by my good fortune. One thing she did give me, a loving scolding which was as far as Emmeline could come to a lecture. "Martha, if you as much as think, 'I wish Emmeline had a cloak too,' and I shall know by the look on your face, I shall be very angry. Remember, I may have felt sad when I had two gowns and you nothing. You care over much for your friends, Martha."

I asked if this was possible.

She said she believed some people were so loving, they bankrupted themselves. "And when their love is spurned by the cold and the unfeeling, then their world becomes a desert. They feel the loss of love more acutely than most of us. I am preaching, I know. But you are so loving and I never want you hurt." She kissed me and we clung to each other for a moment.

We took the train to the station nearest the villages of Great and Lesser Ezekiel, and there, meeting us with a conveyance and a groom, was our own Jamie. "You have filled out," I said, holding him at arms' length. He was taller, pink-cheeked, and the cuffs of his coat did not ride past his wrists.

He talked all the way from the station to our destination. This too was unlike the Jamie we had known. He was more confident, happier, and we looked at each other, Emmeline and I, and rejoiced in it. Jamie said he worked hard, particularly at Latin and Greek and mathematics. His great joy was still reading, and the library at the Big House held over a thousand volumes! "Can you believe that, Martha? I am like a very small bee with a gigantic honey-pot! But Mr Emmett writes me strict lists of what he wishes me to read and I abide by what he says." It was plain he both respected and greatly liked Mr Emmett. "He is teaching me to bowl so that I can join the cricket team here in the village. Next year," Jamie said. "Mr Emmett played for his Oxford College." And so on and so on. Mr Emmett, Mr Emmett. I said, "What about Mr Hatton?"

"He is here sometimes. But Mr Emmett calls him perpetual motion. He dashes from one part of the country to the other when someone of the family needs him. He goes to Yorkshire and to Scotland and to Spain. He is in Spain at the moment," Jamie said. I swallowed my disappointment. I heard Jamie say, "But Mr Emmett is here. He says he will call on you tomorrow. I am to tell him if it is convenient."

"Is it convenient, Emmeline?" I murmured.

We were to stay with Mrs Gudge at her cottage. It was a pretty place with a well in the garden and a huge willow tree. I thought if one Gudge fell out with the other they could take up residence beneath the willow which was as big as a room. Mr Gudge was one of twelve gardeners at the Big House, and Mrs Gudge had worked there before her marriage.

Mrs Gudge was a country version of that Londoner, Mrs Jarrett, as kind and as hard-working, with one fear, that we might rise from the table hungry! She loaded the table with food and her pies and tarts were the best we had ever tasted. I was slightly her favourite because of my good appetite though Emmeline indeed did justice to her meals.

Emmeline took just one day to look well and rested. Was she helped by the presence of Mr Emmett? He did visit us, dwelling-places abounded. "I call the inhabitants here the place. He showed us the houses and cottages of Lower Zeke, then we climbed the hill to Great Ezekiel where the larger dwelling places abounded. "I call the inhabitants here the celestial beings," he told us. "If they knew, I do not think they would argue with me, being convinced that a habitation on the crown of the hill, maybe some degree nearer their Lord, is theirs by right." I surmised here was a man who thought as I did on some aspects of the social scale. He told us there was a garrison town fifteen miles away.

The Big House was of course just that, bigger than any around, the lawns smooth, the trees beautiful. It did not to me look as if a blade of grass grew the wrong way. Well, I thought, twelve gardeners should surely keep it thus. But it seemed to me to be a house, not a home. There should be children on ponies. There should be a nursemaid pushing a new baby in a baby carriage. There should be comings and goings. Nothing except the splendid picture it made of grey stone and shining windows like sightless eyes, and the closed front door. There should be a family, I told myself. A pretty loving wife and mother. There is nothing here for him.

I came to myself to hear Mr Emmett say, "I think it is a bit like a museum. Filled with beautiful things. Mrs Hatton is a collector. But she does not stay anywhere long. I think she likes best to be in France or Italy, particularly when it is the English winter. Rob sees to the estate, here and in Yorkshire. Scotland, too. They expect it of him. And he does not disappoint them."

"When he is married," I heard myself say, "where will he live?"

"I think he likes it here best," Mr Emmett says. Then, "Married? I don't suppose he has time to look at a girl to see if she is pretty—" At which point his eyes strayed to Emmeline. But you have time, I thought.

Is it not a fact that when one has a sore place in one's mouth, the tongue is always exploring there? Thinking of Mr Hatton and marriage, I said, "There must be many pretty young ladies in the neighbourhood?"

"If they don't actually live here, their mamas bring them to stay with relations when they know the family is in residence," said Mr Emmett. "Then it is parties every night."

I asked for this, I told myself. I asked for this heaviness of heart.

"They are not landed gentry, the Hattons," our friend said. "But money is a great leveller. A daughter of a ducal house would not say no, perhaps, to Rob. And I think Mrs Hatton would like a Marquis for Rose Henriette. Lord," he said cheerfully, "what a gossip I turn out to be!" He did not apologize for taking the name of the Lord, either. "Two pretty attentive faces have turned my head," he said. "Made my tongue wag. But believe me, I am fond of Rob and his aunt. I would like to see him happy. And I adore her. I think her fairy tales have bewitched her. She is a Fairy Godmother indeed to so many! And it is they who make it public, not she." He pointed out to us the window of Miss Hatton's room and said she had told him to tell us she hoped to take tea with us before we left.

One day he took us to the sea. It was grey and the waves had white caps on them. Emmeline and he walked ahead of Jamie and me. Jamie asked me if I thought Mr Emmett was attracted by Miss Fairclough. "He is a gentleman," Jamie said, troubled "—and she, though I love her dearly and she is the kindest person, is only—" He stopped, realized who he was talking to, and looked anguished.

"Only a milliner," I finished for him. "Miss Fairclough's father and grandfather were clergymen."

Jamie was delighted to hear it. He looked at the two heads so close together. Mr Emmett had picked up a shell and was showing it to his companion. "Then they are bound to get on famously," Jamie said. "Though I do not suppose they discuss church matters much."

I told him to watch his tongue. Then I did not watch mine. I said, hungry for news, "What does Mr Hatton do in Spain?"

Something to do with wine, Jamie thought. Then he said, "I believe Mr Hatton works as he does to forget much."

"What has he to forget?"

"I have heard that his step-mother once wished aloud that he was dead."

I stared at him. "That is a terrible thing to repeat—"

"I heard it from the servants. I eat there sometimes. They do not always remember I am there. Usually, I read when I eat—"

"And that is wrong too."

"Yes. But if I did not take a book with me they would tease me. Some of the maids are very pert. If I read, or pretend to read, Cook says, 'Leave the lad alone to his studies.' Sometimes they talk so loudly, they come between me and the book—"

"And you listen avidly," I told him. There was silence. He did not say another word. At last, and he had been waiting for it, I said, "Why did they say Mrs Hatton said so awful a thing?"

"Because her sons are dead. She very much loved them, they say. The older was sixteen when he was drowned. The other boy was twelve when he died of a fever. She does not think it fair, perhaps, that both should die and Mr Hatton be alive."

"It is not a question of fairness. It is God's will."

"That is what Cook says. But she says he is a poor lonely bairn. I don't know what bairn is—"

"A boy," I told him.

"Yes. She calls me a good upstanding bairn. Quiet and polite," he grinned.

"With an ear to the ground for maids' gossip."

"Martha," he said very quietly, "you know you want to listen."

I would be honest too. "Yes, I think it a monstrous and unfair thing to say. A terrible thing to live with. To think your mother wishes you were dead so that your brother might be alive."

Jamie said he supposed some mothers did have favourite sons. "They say she cannot bear his presence too long. They say he knows it. I have met the lady once."

"And?" I found I was so angry I trembled.

"I bowed deeply and stared at the hem of her skirt which was dark silk until she passed. I did not look up in case she demanded to know what a boy such as I was doing there. When she passed, I felt as though I had journeyed around an iceberg."

"Does she come to the Big House often?"

"Only to get her recent collection installed," Jamie said. "Porcelain and Eastern carpets and Italian bronzes. That sort of thing. When she comes, they say it is like royalty journeying."

This must be no exaggeration because I learned that almost everyone in Lesser Zeke held Mrs Hatton in impossible awe. But they loved Miss Bertha. She had grown up in these parts. She knew the villagers and they knew her, was how I heard it put. They did not see much of her now, Mrs Gudge said, but it was a strange and fine thing that when there was trouble, illness or death or misfortune, Miss Bertha knew of it straightaway, and did what she could.

One afternoon in our second week Miss Hatton invited Emmeline and me to take tea with her. Mrs

Gudge acted as if the note the groom brought had the Royal coat of arms.

As I followed the footman through the hall and up the stairs, my eyes took in some of the treasures that were here. Marble statues, paintings, bronzes. The balustrade was intricately and wonderfully carved with fruit and flowers. The stairs were uncarpeted but the wood shone with the polish of centuries, I thought, and, being me, thought it would be no use coming flying down here in a hurry. But such a magnificent staircase was meant for a lady to descend it, not for a milliner to run down it. I was impressed, I admit. But if I had spoken, it would have been in that whisper one uses in a museum. This was not a home.

Where the stairs curved there was a magnificent stained-glass window in reds and blues and gold. I would have preferred plain glass through which you might admire the park beyond. You are carping, I told myself. It is not your place to criticize. No. But I knew a home when I saw one.

But once in Miss Bertha's room, all chill was dispelled, mentally and physically. She lay on a sofa, propped against cushions, in a pink gown with a red tartan shawl around her shoulders. Pink and red quarrelled actively. The finishing touch was one of my own blossom-bonnets on her head, daisy-decked. The room was a replica of her room in London, a happy mix of bed, sofa, tables, chairs, flowers and books, writing desk and pen and ink and paper. I ventured to ask after her labours. "I am stuck with *Blue beard*," she confessed. "Try as I may, I can find little sympathy with him." But she did not intend to talk of herself. She wanted to know what we had done, where we had

been. I said at last, "And this morning, we fell in love
with a shop. We have tried hard, every day, to pass it
and find some fault. But we cannot. I gave in, this
morning. I said to Emmeline, 'This is the shop of my
dreams. I can see us setting up a milliners' establishment, here.' And she agreed."

She knew the place. She told us two sisters had kept
it up to a month ago. They had now retired to the
coast. "Their father was a sea captain," said this incor-
rigibly romantic lady, "and they have decided to die
within sound of the fog horns."

"What did they sell?" I asked.

"Things to gladden the children," she said. "Sweets
they made themselves—most wholesome, I enjoyed
them—and they tied them up in pretty cones of striped
paper. They dressed dolls. I bought Rose Henriette
many dolls there, and ordered a complete trousseau for
each. Now you would like to make bonnets there?"

I said I would. Greatly daring, I said I did not believe Emmeline would be with me for long, though.
Emmeline would marry, I said.

Out of the corner of my eye I saw the tea cup, held
in Mr Emmett's right hand, arrested on its way to his
lips. I took pity on him. I said, "Oh, there is no one at
present, as Emmeline would be quick to tell you. But
she is not born to be a spinster."

The cup travelled safely upwards.

"And you think you are?" enquired Miss Hatton.

"Yes, ma'am," I said. "And from choice. A spinster
from choice is a hard nut to crack, to change from her
decision."

"I agree," she said. "I fell in love with the bailiff's
son when I was ten, and with the groom I had when I

was twelve, but from then on I have not wished to marry. I think you would make a very good shopkeeper, Martha."

Should I have been pleased when she said this? The smile and little bow I gave in her direction may have indicated I was pleased. But the word "shopkeeper", seemed to toll in my mind, sitting here in this room, in this great rich house, which was his home.

Jamie handed round cakes and biscuits with great aplomb. It was not difficult to be at ease with this sweet dear little person. I felt regretful when I wished her goodbye. Perhaps it was presumptuous on my part but I think I looked upon her as a friend. Mr Emmett and Jamie accompanied us across the park and back to the village.

The next morning, our last there, we went to take one more look at the little shop I had fallen in love with. It was a sweet Regency gem, and I was more certain than ever that if a miracle happened and Emmeline and I might rent this place, we would be happy here and do well. A miracle, indeed. I sighed and peered farther through the window.

"A bonnet at one side," I dreamed. "One of our stylish velvet and feathers and rich satin ribbon bonnets. The sort we sell to the mamas of the chits I make the blossom-bonnets for. An Indian shawl draped carelessly—oh, but carefully carelessly, to show its colours and softness. Perhaps a pair of pretty embroidered gloves. And the sign: *Fairclough et Cie.*"

"Why not *Bates et Cie?*" said the kind Emmeline.

"Because it has not the same ring," I said, truthfully.

I was teasing but I was surprised at her reaction. She came close to me and looked into my face and said, in her soft voice, "Martha, why do you put yourself down? It is a habit of yours. Other people do not put you down—"

"You do not know," I said, savagely twisting my arm away from the touch of her hand.

She said, "I sometimes think, and I grieve for it, that you have suffered some cruel act, Martha. I am not asking you to tell me. I cannot comfort you, I know. You have pride and do not wish to share what happened. Only remember, you are a person greatly loved."

I made to interrupt but for once she was stubborn. "Everyone loves you who knows you. Mr Dee and Mr Diss. Dear Mrs Jarrett. Jamie adores you. I love you. Madame Ferrier seeks your well-being—"

"I am a thorn in her flesh."

"Only because you are human and act first and think after, but she knows there is not a mean thought in your mind, and you would not act meanly. Why, Martha, you goose, did you not guess she bought your dress and cloak especially for you? There was no friend exactly your size. I am certain of it. The dress is quite new, and the cloak. Martha, please believe—"

"What am I to believe?"

"You are, as I say, a person others seek out and choose. When you give your heart, the man will be the most fortunate of men. I know you say you will never marry. But you will marry and have children and live happily—"

"*Ever after,*" I concluded. "I will not. I say I will not marry and I mean it—"

"So we must understand," the voice said behind us. "Most of the village would hear if they were near." But there was such laughter in his voice I could only smile in welcome and in the joy of seeing him, the wide smile he had once remarked upon. Mr Emmett accompanied him. Jamie, he said, was at his lessons. "I have given him an exercise which will keep him quiet for some time." I would not have been surprised if this was not to give Mr Emmett the chance to be alone for one last time with Emmeline.

"Has any man importuned you to marry him?" Mr Hatton asked me. "You are so vehement, you must have taken against him."

"It is my opinion," I said.

"And she stands by it," Emmeline murmured.

"Are you," the curate asked, "of the same opinion?"

"No," I said for her. "She will marry as one of those whose price is above rubies."

Before I could gather strength, and no doubt continue with the one hundredth-and-twenty-seventh psalm, the happy man with the quiver full of children, Emmeline panicked and said she must return to the cottage. Mr Emmett of course went with her.

His friend and I were left outside the little empty shop. "Dick and I spent pocket-money on toffee apples here," he said. "Dick was my step-brother. We were great friends. I miss him. Now Rose Henriette was always sensible. She would not eat sweets. To save her teeth."

"She need not have worried," I said coldly. "Her teeth are perfect. So is she. A perfect example of a young lady of fashion." I said, before I could stop myself, "We see many where we work."

"I wonder. I half guessed. My sister was—abrupt

with you, when you called at the house in Mount Street?"

"I was to blame," I said. "I called at the wrong door. It is the servents' entrance for milliners. I forgot, for the moment."

He apologized and I, I suppose, came to my senses. It was not his fault. Indeed, I would have put it down to the bad manners of a spoiled chit, a word Emmeline did not like me using but which I derived satisfaction from spitting out, if my own sister had not been the audience. But he knew nothing of this. He said, "I was disappointed when you did not come but sent Miss Fairclough."

And again the ghost of my sister laughed in my face as I thought about it, "I could not come, sir."

"Of course not," he said, and his face was dark but whether with anger or shame for his sister I could not tell. He said, "My sister is pretty and spoiled. She is the only one left to my step-mother. You may imagine how she dotes on her. Not giving her too many treats, but she is my step-mother's life."

I could only nod. I did not know what to say. I only had a vague feeling that this man was hurt as perhaps I had been hurt, and I wished to God I could think of some way to heal it for him. He asked me why the shop appealed to me, and I was glad to change the conversation. I said I supposed most young milliners longed for a place of their own.

"Like schoolteachers?" he said. "Julian wishes to teach. No doubt before long he will wish for his own school."

Emmeline, a headmaster's wife? I considered it. Yes, it would do. She would grace this too with as much sweetness and charm and expertise as a wife of the rectory. In fact, I thought being a headmaster's wife much better. Small boys would love Emmeline and turn to her when they missed their mamas as they must, sent to school so young. I thought it barbaric to send them off so young. I did not think I could do it.

"Where are you now?" I heard him say.

And I laughed. "Oh sir, it is what Madame says. *Martha, do not day-dream.*"

"You indulge in dreams? I suppose every girl does—"

I did not suppose Rose Henriette had to day-dream. But I said, worriedly, "I think I am progressing from dreams to thinking of miracles. I had better stop."

"Why stop? Faith removes mountains," he teased.

"But it will not pour into my lap sufficient sovereigns to rent or buy this shop. Sir," I said, "do you know the owner?"

"Yes," he said and laughed. I turned scarlet. Of course, he was the owner. Everything was spoiled. I had told him I was expecting a miracle. It might seem as if I begged him to make it possible, admitted we had no money, would be grateful if he made it easy for us to come here.

I muttered I must return to Emmeline. As I turned, he held me by the arm and made me face him. He said, "What you are thinking is unworthy of you and of me. If a miracle does happen and you wish to come here, I am certain my man of business will arrange a lease." Then he wished me good day and left.

I had been put in my place, I thought. Strangely, I felt I deserved it. If anyone else had done it, I would have been angry and self-justifying. But he was right. I had not meant to beg and he knew it. How could I put such thoughts into his mind?

How indeed? Each time I saw him I fell deeper in love.

Ten

We returned to London loaded with what I called the fruits of the earth. A goose, a ham, nuts and apples. Flowers and honey and jam.

Mrs Jarrett cooked the goose and invited Messrs Dee and Diss to the meal which was superb. The goose cooked with sage and onion stuffing, a gravy made with its giblets. Potatoes and vegetables. A boiled apple pudding. Nuts and apples to follow. Mr Dee provided wine and Mr Diss a cheese.

When we returned to work we gave Madame Ferrier a bunch of flowers and a round wicker basket filled with apples we had industriously polished.

I had been back a week when I received a letter to call upon a firm of solicitors in Lincoln's Inn. "What have I done?" I asked Emmeline who, sensible creature, told me to look on the other side, that I might have been left a fortune.

Not a fortune. But I had been left a legacy of one hundred pounds.

Madame Ferrier was at home with a chill so I must ask Miss Moses for time off to call where I had been bidden. Grudgingly she gave it.

The solicitor's name was Redding. He was a tall, ruddy-faced, smiling young man who looked in the best of health and spirits. He begged me to take a chair, remarked on the filthy day, as he described it, wondered aloud why we did not all emigrate, we Londoners, to the South Seas, then came to the point. *I had been left a legacy of one hundred pounds*. I said immediately he must have the wrong Martha Bates. He smiled harder and said no. "Niece of Miss Dorcas Bigby of Pond Cottage in the village of East Frobisher in the county of Kent? Of course you are. We got your address from Miss Dorcas's one-time maid, Sarah Prendergast. Don't pretend you do not know Sarah Prendergast."

I must write to her more often, I thought.

He explained, "When your aunt, Miss Dorcas, was young she had an admirer, one Toby Vole. Mr Vole left to make his fortune in North America. He never married. He has no brothers or sisters or family. He left the bulk of the money to charity but he did remember his one-time sweetheart and left Miss Dorcas Bigby the sum of one hundred pounds. If Miss Dorcas Bigby was dead, the money was to go to her niece, the child she had brought up when her sister died."

"I never knew of Mr Vole," I said.

"I believe he asked her to marry him," Mr Redding told me, "but you were already in her care and she refused the good man. But he remembered your name, you see. Martha Bates."

Aunt Dorcas, I thought, why did you refuse him? We might have gone with him to America. You would have been happy. I wiped the tears off my cheeks.

"Great, ain't it?" beamed Mr Redding. "Nicest way to start a rotten week, telling a young girl she has inherited a hundred pounds. What will you do with it? Start by buying a bonnet, eh?"

"I make bonnets," I said.

"A holiday, then?"

"I have just returned from a holiday. I hope to open my own shop," I said.

"Part of our nation of shopkeepers, what? Where were you thinking of starting up?" When I told him, he said, "The place where Rob Hatton lives for some of the time? Nice place. Prettiest girls for miles. I'm always telling Rob what a lucky dog he is. He can take his pick of beauties like picking apples from a tree." He stopped, remembered where he was, and said, "Yes, well. The money will be deposited in your bank, Miss Bates."

I did not say I had no bank. I was saying nothing in the negative at this moment. I only said, "You will write to me, sir, and confirm all this?"

"Can't take it in, eh? One hundred pounds." He rose, and saw me out. It was my first acquaintance with the law and I could scarcely be forgiven for thinking them a jolly lot.

I told no one about what had happened but that same night I wrote a letter and posted it. When I got a reply—and my faith had been so strong I was certain that he must still be at the Big House and so not far from London and I would get a reply—I was indeed to call at Mount Street on Sunday morning.

I put completely from my mind the last stupid thoughts I had and which he recognized when we said goodbye in the village street. I only wanted his advice out of all the people I knew, and I knew he would give it.

This time we went into the library. There was a roaring fire in the grate. The curtains were drawn, though it was noon, against the rain and the cold outside. The room was cheerful and welcoming. I sat on a chair near the fire and he sent for chocolate and biscuits. Now, though, I only wanted the chocolate. For a moment I recollected the first time when my hand had strayed, not once, towards the sweets in the dish.

I warmed my hands around the cup of chocolate. He kicked the logs with his foot so they blazed harder. He said I looked frozen. "It is cold outside," I agreed. And I said ridiculously, "It is cold in the country?"

"Frost," he said. "Jamie is learning to skate."

Then I came to my senses and realized I must not waste his time. I told him about my legacy and he was obviously delighted. "And now, you wish to leave London and start up on your own?"

"Yes, sir. May I rent the shop? I am certain," I said, no doubt sounding pompous, "you are not asked often about such a small piece of property but I do not know your man of business yet and I do know you—"

"My man of business is very clever and very kind," he said. "You will like him. What else worries you?"

"Two things. Of course I wish to take Emmeline with me. She and I are as close as sisters. I should hate to be parted from her and I think she wishes to come."

He said gravely, "I am certain she would wish to live there. She would be a most devout churchgoer."

"I think she loves him," I said.

"And I think he loves her. Jamie thinks it too. Julian has taken to mooning about which is something he has never done. I cannot think of anyone save Miss Fairclough. There are many girls around who look his way. Their mamas would be delighted—"

I found myself saying aloud, "The prettiest girls in the county."

"Where did you hear that?"

"Mr Redding described them thus." But I said no more about the pretty girls because Mr Redding, when he said it, had not been discussing Mr Emmett's choice.

"I believe they are pretty," he said and my heart felt a twinge of jealousy. "My step-sister invites them to the house in summer. They make me feel old."

"Old?" I echoed. "You are just twenty-eight."

Astonished, he asked how I knew this.

Now I am in trouble, deep as ever, I told myself. I had tried hard lately to keep out of trouble. I had copied no one's bonnet for myself. I had kept a curb on my tongue until now. I had to confess. "A girl in the workroom is from Yorkshire, sir. I think her family works on your father's estate. We—we talked, I fear. She said you were born in eighteen hundred and thirty-four," I said, not above a whisper.

Oh, he had a right to be angry. He, a gentleman, to be the object of gossip in the workroom. I looked at him. He was biting his lip not to laugh. Reprieve, again. He was indeed the kindest man. I said, sighing, "We talk a great deal when we are at work."

"Young milliners do not have the prerogative of gossip," he said. "How old are you?" I said my birthday had been the week before. Two days after we returned from the country. I was twenty years of age.

"Did you celebrate?"

"Lord, no, sir," I said. "We had four mourning orders and a lot to do. The fog is wiping out the upper classes at a great rate. But Mrs Jarret cooked a goose dinner for us which was a treat. Then Emmeline would give me her second-best pair of gloves as a gift. She wished to give me her best pair but I would have none of it. I am murder on gloves," I said simply.

He asked me to excuse him, left the room but returned very soon. He was holding in his hand a carved ivory figure, no more than a few inches high. A little sleeping angel, exquisite and beautiful. So delicately carved, with its head on its arm and its wings folded, I gave a little cry of joy when I saw it. I had never in my life seen anything so lovely. "A birthday gift," he said. "I should have given you a dozen pairs of gloves, as well."

"*Oh, no, sir! This is beautiful—*" I said, and hoped that he could see in my face and hear in my tone how I felt. I held it for the moment to my cheek. "I will keep it always. Tiny as it is, it will guard over me, I know it will." I had to add, "I need an angel. For I do not think Dorcas can manage on her own."

"Now," he said, "about your friend. I think you should ask her to go with you. What are the lines in *The Dream*?" he said, "Jamie would know. '*So we grew together—*' "

" '*Like a double cherry, seeming parted, But yet an*

union in partition—' " I said, scorning the thought of Jamie.

" *'Two lovely berries moulded on one stem,'* " he concluded. I coughed. I said, "Then there is Madame Ferrier. Emmeline is a good milliner. I have my flashes of inspiration. I would not like Madame to think that we were leaving her with too short staff. I value her good opinion."

"And you know that if things were different and Madame was young and had this urge to work for herself and the chance to do it, she would take the chance as you want to do."

Even so, when I had my interview with my employer I was very nervous. She was fair. She said she understood and that to leave at the start of the New Year, which is what she thought we would do, gave her time to take on two more girls. "I have a long list, always," she said. "I think you and Miss Fairclough will work well together. Heed her," she ordered me. "She will think things out to a conclusion where you will rush in." Then she became businesslike. She gave me the names of purveyors of ribbons and silks and flowers and shapes and all the rest we needed for bonnet-making. She said she would personally write to them. "So see you pay your bills promptly," she told me.

I said of course we would.

"If you are unfortunate enough to attract bad payers yourself," she told me, "show them no mercy. *Dun them.* They are the poison of establishments such as ours. Do not listen to the fashionable woman who demands a substantial amount taken off the price of the bonnet because she is *seen everywhere,* and will therefore advertise your handiwork. If she is seen everywhere, she will tell no one where she gets her clothes. If they will not pay, send the account to their husband or protector."

I felt a hundred years old and I owlishly nodded. By the time she listed the pitfalls, I should have cried it off. Instead, I was exhilarated.

Only then did I tell Emmeline about my legacy, my talks with Mr Hatton and with Madame. "I have told her I am leaving," I said. "I said we would like to go together. That is right, is it not? But of course, I have not given your notice in."

"But of course I am coming, and thank you, my love, for wanting me," she said, and swept me into her arms and hugged and kissed me. We foolishly shed some tears of joy.

Mrs Jarret, that philosophical soul, knew enough about lodgers to know they came and went. They were not all like Dee and Diss. We bought her, as a parting gift, the painting of a shipwreck in oils which she had long admired in a window. She was very pleased, telling us nothing stirred her like a good wreck. Already, Madame had two girls to take our places. Mrs Jarret said that if we ever came to London, and she would be desolate if she never saw either of us again, we were to stay with her and not waste money on hotels.

Business was in hand between Mr Hatton's man and one Martha Bates. I signed a lease to rent the little shop in the High Street in the village of Lesser Ezekiel, and my hand did not shake when I signed.

Our last day came. Madame wished us goodbye. So—sniff—did Miss Moses. The girls gave us a large red satin pin cushion, lace-edged, with the letters E and M entwined in silk.

Why is it, when you leave people for good, there is not one among them whom you dislike?

We left London the first week in January, 1863. As on the day I arrived, the city was black and horrid with fog and rain.

It rained in Lesser Ezekiel, too. But somehow it seemd cleaner. It was cleaner, I thought. There was no soot there.

We would stay with Mrs Gudge until our rooms behind the shop were ready. We hoped this would not take long, not that Mrs Gudge's house was not comfortable—did we not have first-hand experience of it?—but we were like children impatient to get into the new house. Mrs Gudge, like Mrs Jarrett, treated us as daughters and was kindness itself. We were unexpectedly lucky because a family she knew were leaving for the New World. They were going to Pennsylvania and not taking their furniture with them. Mrs Gudge told us we might go and view it, and make a bid for it which we did. So, without much trouble, we furnished the kitchen which was also our sitting-room, and two bedrooms upstairs. The little room behind the shop was our workroom. Our own rooms were very simple. "We are here," Emmeline said, sternly, "to work, not to entertain. For the first year, it is the shop which is our prime concern. So we will spend on furnishing that rather than the back rooms."

"You will entertain Mr Emmett in the kitchen?" I teased. She said calmly that she would. I believed her. There was not one shred of false pride in her.

I looked at her, at this moment, tall and slim, her dark hair in a low chignon on her neck, caught in a pretty snood of chenille with ribbons at each side. She wore a large apron over her working dress. Her cheeks were flushed and she was singing. I had never seen her look more beautiful. Since I was what I was, of course I immediately wondered what I should do, how I should feel, if things did not go right? What if the ladies did not care for our bonnets? What if all the money trickled away while we sat waiting for the shop door to open and a customer to enter? Would Madame take us back?

I heard Emmeline's calm voice. "I know where you are now, Martha. You have gone through the bankruptcy court. You are begging Madame to take me back, at least. You are a goose," she said, waving a duster at me. "We have not started yet, let alone closed."

Well, I thought, you can always marry the curate so Madame will only have to take me back.

When the boxes came with the materials for our work, we set to that very night. We worked hard and decided to open the shop on March the first. We decided we would not open until we had a fair stock of bonnets. There could be nothing worse than a lady saying, "What else have you to offer?" and we would say, "No more, I fear. You have gone through all six."

Mr Emmett did not call often. He told us he would not come because we were so busy. Jamie, though, we ordered about in his spare time like a kitchen boy. "Paint there—" "Scrub here—" "Drive nails in this." He took messages, went on errands, and drove in the cart to the station to collect boxes for us. He loved it, I know. It was kind of the Hatton family to take him into their house and to educate him. But when he came to us, to our little shop in the High Street, this was his home.

We enjoyed a bedroom each, Emmeline and I. She sewed curtains for each room. I bought rag rugs from a friend of Mrs Gudge who made them for two shillings each. Emmeline had in her room a picture of her father and mother and her little brother. I had a painting of Dorcas and her sister, my mother, when they were young girls. Ringlets, arms entwined. I did not show Emmeline my little ivory angel. It was the only thing I kept from her. But at night, when I had knelt and said my prayers, and I prayed for him, every night, I got into bed and reached for it from beneath my pillow, and held it for a minute to my face. Like a benediction. Then I put it back beneath my pillow.

We shared the satin pin cushion.

We opened the shop when daffodils were gold in gardens, buds and catkins on the willow trees, and robins in the garden. Spring was almost here and we told ourselves it was the perfect time for us.

We did not, after all, put *Fairclough et Cie* on the board which swung from its arm above the doorway to the shop. It said, simply, *Bonnets*. I had an idea Mr Hatton would approve. That first day, we displayed two bonnets in the window, a stylish black velvet and satin ribbon trimmed with jet and feathers, and one of my blossom bonnets, in ruched silk yellow as the daffodils.

We did not sell one bonnet, all week, and by the end of the week, though Emmeline still sang around the place, I found there were times when I could not look at her.

Ladies called, examined the stock, sat on the chair

in front of the mirror and tried on a bonnet, tried more than one, asked the price, and left.

So they did know we were here. On the opposite side of the High Street was an attractive and very busy tea shop. At eleven in the morning it was filled with ladies whose carriages had brought them from Great Ezekiel for a morning's visit to the shops of Lesser Zeke. Here they would be the scourge of the grocer, if they felt so inclined, buy some lace or ribbons at the haberdashery, and meet their friends for tea. I had thought our shop splendidly situated in relation to the tea shop. When they had imbibed, they might cross the street and look in the window and perhaps see some bonnet or hat they approved of. It did not happen.

Emmeline and I wore our smartest bonnets to morning service on Sunday. She wore a Glengarry in tartan with a cockade at one side. I, for once, was the more demure in a velvet bonnet of a tawny shade with clusters of rowan berries on each side and velvet streamers. "*Regard us—*" I silently urged the females of the congregation. "Break the commandment. I will myself take all your sins. *But covet our bonnets.* Tell yourselves you must have one like it."

I was punished for my presumption. God is not mocked. Monday came and no one entered the shop.

Eleven

On Tuesday morning I saw from the shop the Hatton carriage driven up the street. In the street the ladies jostled and pushed to see where it would stop and who the occupant was. It was like sycophants trying to get close to royalty.

The coachman sprang down and opened the door. Solomon Figg helped Miss Bertha alight, then helped her towards the front door of our shop. Solomon Figg was the largest man I had ever seen, one of the handsomest, and the most gentle. He was a man without one mean thought in his soul, I think. He was black and came from the West Indies. He loved serving Miss Bertha. When she said, forgetting his tender heart, "When I am dead, Solomon—" a tear would roll down his cheek.

I opened the door, greeted her and gave a low curtsey. "Good morning, child," she said but she was not ready yet to enter the shop. She acknowledged the ladies' greetings by calling their names. "Lady Dalrymple—Miss Foster—Miss Smith-Brown and sister Gladys —Mrs Archdeacon Gigg. Lady Gosling, I did not know you had returned from Scotland." Like summer rain on a garden for the faces, when named, beamed their pleasure.

Miss Hatton, pointing to the sign outside our shop, said, "My *protégées*. Martha Bates and Emmeline Fairclough. Both served with Madame Ferrier of Hanover Square. But of course you know Ferrier. The only milliner in London. Two of her best girls. She was not anxious to let them come here. You have already chosen a bonnet, Eugenia? And you, Clara, and your dear sister, the vicar's wife who I see is staying with you. Of course you have," Miss Bertha said. "How could you not have been tempted."

It was as good as a play and I, who loved things theatrical, was entranced.

"I am here to buy six bonnets," Miss Bertha said. "Now, Eugenia, before you tell me six is excessive, I will tell you I cannot agonize over dear Martha's creations. They are all so exquisite. Emmeline too has the elegant touch. I always say Martha's bonnets are for the garden party, Emmeline's for a wedding at St George's. St George's, Hanover Square—" with wicked emphasis. "In London, I recalled telling Martha Bates I wished to buy her. Her exclusive designs, you understand. I was so touched when, having obtained her legacy, she decided to come here. Oh yes, not a poor girl by any means. Martha creates bonnets because it interests her. So now," she continued, "we shall have no excuse for looking dowdy here in the country. For I always say," raking her audience with a shrewd eye, "one can tell in an instant a London bonnet from a country one!"

When she was in the shop and sitting on our velvet-covered chair, she said, "I am certain they will be in here by tomorrow at least." Then she really did choose six bonnets. When we bade her goodbye, we saw the ladies, clustered around the tea shop entrance, count the boxes.

On Easter Sunday, there were nine of our bonnets on the church-going ladies.

And so the weeks passed from Easter to Whitsun. We sent hampers of country fare up to Mrs. Jarrett and I wrote to Sarah telling her what had happened. We did not see much of Mr Emmett though Jamie called almost every day. Mr Emmett was taking the place of the curate here for some months. The curate was sickly and was at home being fussed over by five sisters and an adoring mother. "He is stronger than he looks," Mr Emmett had told us, "or that lot would have killed him long ago. They hover so far over him it is a wonder he can breathe."

Mr Emmett, fair and young and handsome, was a favourite with the mamas of Great Ezekiel. If he wished, he could have gone to parties and gatherings each evening. Sometimes the ladies, trying on our bonnets, gossiped about him as if we were not visible. We were told that the Frobisher girl and the Dalrymple niece were neck and neck in their advances. We heard that Lady Gosling's graddaughter was bound to catch him. It is a pernicious habit of the loud-mouthed and ruder type of customer to talk through and around the person serving her as if the latter is not there. Real

ladies never do it. When these ladies did it I would agonize for Emmeline. Did she feel jealous, hopeless, did
she fear that Mr Emmett might be 'caught' there
among the scented pretty traps for such as he in Great
Ezekiel? I never asked her.

Before the end of the London Season, Mrs Hatton
brought Rose Henriette down to the country. Gossip
told us it was because the young lady had enjoyed the
Season too much, there in London. Gossip said she
was headstrong and spoiled, that even a lady as
strong-willed as Mrs Hatton had her work cut out to
keep Rose Henriette in hand. Gossip said that the fortune hunters were round her like bees round a honey
pot. In particular, one handsome gentleman called
Comstock. Bevan Comstock. When I heard it I thought
if he had not been christened thus he would have had
to adopt such a name since it was perfect for a fortune
hunter. I had never met such a man. I imagined him
tall and dark, with black moustache and a dashing way
with him. A romantic Spanish-looking man, bold.
When I did meet Mr Comstock, he was slight, fair,
quiet, with a beautiful speaking voice and exquisite
manners. He might have been a clerk in Holy Orders.

One morning, Mrs Hatton descended on us in the
shop, and this was the word for the way she condescended to enter, address us, say what she wanted
and leave. I remembered Jamie's description of her as
an iceberg and it was true. She was elegantly dressed in
a silk gown and a shawl that must have been Paris
bought. Her bonnet, too. This was a French bonnet,
not one in the French mode. Her gloves . . . oh, I
thought, her gloves. They were the softest silk, the
shade of her dress, not a wrinkle anywhere, with little

tassels hanging from the wrist. They say you can tell a
lady by her gloves, and this was a very rich lady. She
told us her sister-in-law had mentioned the shop. She
wanted us to send bonnets to the house. For her maid.
Mrs Hatton wished to give her maid the gift of a bonnet. Emmeline said, in her sweet soft voice, "Thank
you, madam. We shall be very pleased to send a selec-
tion up to the house. Perhaps, if you might give us the
colouring of your maid—her height—indeed, her age."
But even Emmeline faltered and stopped before that
cold gaze. Mrs Hatton said she had no idea how old
her maid was, turned and left us.

"Jamie will tell us about the girl," Emmeline said.
"Martha, do not be vexed. We served ladies like this in
London." I was not vexed with Mrs Hatton except that
she was step-mother to Robert. She appeared a cold,
unfriendly, unfeeling woman, and I remembered what
Jamie told us he had heard in the servants' hall, that
she could not forgive Robert for being alive when her
two sons were dead.

I had not seen Mr Hatton since that morning in
Mount Street, and I thought sometimes, depressed, I
had seen him more often in town than here on his
buy, too. We had nothing to do, Bella and I, so we
The curtseys, when Mrs Hatton left to make her way
doorstep.
to her carriage, the bows and the inclined heads, the
hats of the gentlemen off in a flash, it really was like
royalty. All except the cheer as she passed.

Next day Rose Henriette called on us, with friend.

I curtseyed to both young ladies but my sister did
not glance my way. Rose Henriette wore pink muslin,
prettily edged with lace to match, her bonnet tied with
pink ribbons. My pretty twin, to offset her nasturtium-

coloured hair, wore a white, white dress, white bonnet, white lace parasol. Of the two, Rose Henriette looked the more human. My sister was a fashion plate. Once, I looked up and caught her looking at me, hating me, wishing me dead, I was sure.

"It is you?" said the young Miss Hatton, with a surpushy young girl. Aunt Bertha ordered me to buy something here so that it might stir the bumpkins to have come to look at your stock. I expect it is not worth looking at," with a sudden languid adopting of what she must have thought was a world-weary air. prise I knew was genuine. "The upstart milliner? The You are very young in your mind, I thought, whatever you think.

"Arabella?" Rose Henriette said. My sister only shrugged, stood by the window and disassociated herself from us. "I want nothing," she said. "Not in this place."

"Now that is snobbish of you," chuckled young Miss Hatton. "Remember the Christian teaching we suffered at school. Do unto others. Act well to the lower orders."

"Why must I?" my sister retorted.

"Goodness knows, they will always dislike us for what we are and what we have," Miss Hatton said, merrily. "Come along, milliner, show us what you have to offer," She was deliberately riling me but I would not rise to it.

Emmeline came in and must have recognized at once something was amiss. But she smiled and was polite as a good shopkeeper should be, and I thought, in her dark cerise gown with matching snood on her black hair, tall and thin and with creamy skin, she was as elegant as any rich man's daughter. Miss Hatton carelessly introduced herself, and I felt a spasm of terror. I thought, "Please, Lord, do not let her say, 'And this is my friend, Miss Bigby.' It is not a common name. Emmeline knows it was Dorcas's name. I will swear that there must be many Bigbys but I would prefer not to have to do it for Emmeline is shrewd. Please, Lord, help me."

Of course Miss Hatton did not introduce her friend, not to milliners. Impudently she repeated that they were both bored, this morning, and had come to turn over our stock though she knew they would find nothing to suit them. Emmeline said they were welcome to look at the bonnets on display. She said to me, "Martha, the box is ready to take to Lady Dalrymple—"

"Do you serve that old hag?" Rose Henriette enquired. "A face like a horse. I should have thought a straw hat with holes for ears, such as donkeys wear, would do her."

When I returned from Lady Dalrymple's house, they had gone. Miss Hatton had, perhaps to her surprise, found something she liked. A country bonnet of plaited Italian straw. Her friend bought nothing.

When my uncle Bigby came to the shop, Emmeline was in Great Ezekiel for the afternoon, and I was grateful for it. I knew why he had come. My sister had written to say I was here and ordered him to remove me. When he demanded to know why I was there, what I was doing, I said I was earning an honest living.

"How did you come by the money to start up?" he demanded.

I would not tell him about the legacy. I did not want

him to know of Dorcas. I told him that was my business but I was not expecting his explanation which was that some man had set me up here since this was the kind of girl I was. It was so pitiful I even smiled, which of course enraged him further.

"My daughter is a guest at the Hatton house," he said.

I nodded.

"I want you to get out of here. If they ever knew who you are—"

"Believe me," I said, "I shall not tell them. The episode that day at your house fills me with shame each time I think of it, shame for you that you acted as you did to your own niece. I admit I left your house feeling wretched but since then I have met good, kind people—"

"And taken them in by your sly looks and your lies—"

"I tell lies," I admitted. "When someone asks me if I have family, I say no, that I am alone in the world. I am ashamed to admit I have you for an uncle."

"I will get you out of here," he shouted. "You—and my beloved Bella not a few miles from one another. I will see that the Hattons know what kind of girl you are."

"If you do lie about me," I told him, "then I will tell the truth. I will tell Mr Robert Hatton. I will tell his aunt, Miss Bertha—"

"You do not know them—"

"I would not bank on that. It is from them that Emmeline Fairclough and I have derived greatest kindness. Miss Bertha describes us as her *protégées*. She would not care to hear how you treated me—"

"Did Hatton give you the money to set up this place?"

A red mist of anger seemed to come into my mind. I picked up a wooden stand that was on the low table near me. We used it for displaying bonnets. I picked it up and advanced on him. Anyone watching would have thought it good enough for Mackays. He retreated like a rat against the wall. Then I put down the stand and laughed. I said, "No. Mr Hatton did not give me the money. But if you do not leave here, I shall add what you have just said to other things I might tell him—"

He looked cunning. He said, "You will have no witness. It is just the two of us. No one will believe you."

He was contemptible. I said, "They will believe me when they know how you first treated me."

"For Bella's sake," he said, and I could hardly believe my ears. Why should I do anything for her sake? "If they knew you are her sister, she would be a laughing-stock. She would be asked nowhere. How much money do you want to go away and stay away?"

For answer I picked the stand up again. If anyone came in, at this moment, they would be astounded. One little man cowering against a wall, and I threatening him with a display stand.

"I cannot wipe guilt and fear out of your mind, nor your wife's," I said. "But believe me when I say I have as little wish as Bella of being known as her sister. That desire—and it was great and deep—died the morning I came to you. I will tell no one. If she cannot bear the sight of me, the thought of me here, then she must refuse her invitations to the Hatton house."

"Do not mention Bella's name," he shouted. "You are no sister of hers—"

"Then why do you worry so? Uncle," I said, wickedly, "you must go back to London with only my word that I will keep your secret. All your money, your position, your friends, nothing can guard you,. seemingly, from fearing that I will let out your secret. I can only tell you I will not. Do not come here again. You have heard my last word."

"You are a wicked, evil girl," he shouted, "and will end up in hell where you deserve to be!"

I hoped not for if I did it was certain he and his ilk would be there.

He rushed out, colliding with Emmeline as she came in. He did not apologize and when she asked me, astonished, who he was, I said, "Someone who had lost his way and asked my help. I gave him instructions."

The next week there was to be a party at the Big House. Most of the families of Great Ezekiel were invited. Anyone who was left out would no doubt pack her bags and go away to the other end of the country for a month. We were ordered to make evening headdresses for at least six ladies, we pored over the fashion journals for the latest caps, then, when we showed them, were told no, the lady in question wanted the sort of cap she usually wore. Two ladies, known for their meanness, asked us to unstitch the lace from their old caps and make it up again.

I was summoned by Miss Bertha and ordered to make a head-dress for her. "I shall not be at the party," she said. "But I will not be deprived of one of your confections. What have you in mind for me, child?" First though she had to know what we were making for some of the ladies. "Two new lace head-dresses," I said. "Two head-dresses with the lace un-stitched and stitched again—"

She knew the ladies in question. "That lace would find its way to any party in the neighbourhood. And a turban of shot silk with an egret feather pinned by a clasp her grandfather was given by a sultan, some years ago, for Mrs Gooch?"

"No need for you to stir from your couch, ma'am," I agreed. "Now, for your bonnet—" I looked at her, eyes narrowed, lips pursed. "Like Rembrandt before his easel," she said. I looked at the pale drawn little face with the all too discernible marks of pain, at the shadows beneath the eyes, at the mouse-like hair. And I looked and took comfort in, was warmed by the wide happy smile. I remembered that never once had I heard this lady complain of illness or pain. She is, I told myself truthfully, a really great lady.

"I have a piece of apricot silk," I said. "I shall fash-ion tiny apricots with dark green velvet leaves. I shall make miniature black-eyed Susans—you know, ma'am, the great stand-by of cottage gardens. I shall join pieces of lace with strips of black velvet. Silver rib-bon—"

She gave me a deep happy sigh, and she said, "I am so glad we met."

Greatly daring, I asked what Mrs Hatton might wear.

"She has a new gown from Paris which Great Eze-kiel has not seen yet. It is green so she will wear her emeralds," said Miss Hatton, easily.

"And Miss Rose Henriette?"

"You have reminded me, Martha, that my niece

wishes to see you when you have finished here. She wishes you to design her head-dress."

My heart sank.

But dutifully, as a milliner should, I went to Miss Rose Henriette's sitting-room. My sister was riding, this morning, so I was fortunate not to meet her. Miss Rose Henriette came immediately to the point. "You will make for me something better than anyone else will wear. My aunt says you are inspired. I think that is foolish. But I quite like my aunt and I said you might try to please me. What do you suggest, milliner?"

I damped down my anger for I did not even think that now she was consciously trying to upset me. Then she said, "Lord, I am bored out of town. I had such a richness of parties there. One every evening if mama had allowed me to go. But she is all starch with some of the other mothers. Mama is so rich, she wears her money like a—like a—" She foundered for the word.

"Like a carapace?" I said.

"What is that?"

I told her the shell of a crab or tortoise, and because I knew the word and she did not, and perhaps because the word fitted, I could see it annoyed her. I saw it when the blue eyes became slits and a faint flush came into her cheeks. "So? It is an educated milliner. Where did you learn such words?"

I told her I had taught school for a short time with my aunt. She trilled with laughter at the idea. Then she said, "Are you in love, milliner? No? Not with some grocer smelling of cheese, twisting screws of tea, weighing potatoes?"

"No," I said.

"You dream perhaps of a Prince Charming to ride

into your life and help you escape? I believe you girls read a lot of silly novels. Do you know my brother? Yes? Someone like him, then? All the girls fall in love with him. Silly Mary Cummings had to be sent to Ireland because she chased him. Belinda Greenhill told me she died for love of him. Robert, the wretch, knows they love him and is polite, no more. He is hard-hearted as a stone. I tell him," she said, "he must have some little mistress tucked away."

I longed to ask what he said in reply but I stood, listening, giving nothing away. I heard her say, "Though he can be soft-hearted. He will try to help most people though they bore him half to death."

I told myself not to think of the letter I had written asking him for advice nor the morning he had come up to town to give it to me. I heard Rose Henriette say, "It is a nuisance, my brothers' dying. Mama is inclined to over-protect me. And she fair hates Rob, cannot bear to have him around." Then, incredibly, "Why are we discussing my family? Why are we not deciding what you will make me for the party?"

"If you will describe your dress, ma'am."

Blue silk. A crinoline. Blue roses at the neck and lying on the three folds of the skirt. "Or I may wear my pink—"

"Why do you choose such simple colours?" I asked, coolly.

Her face flamed. "You are impertinent! I like blue. Have you no eyes? I am fair in colouring. You are a dolt not to see that. Did they not teach you a fair lady should wear soft colours?" I stood my ground until, at last and reluctantly, she said, "What colour do you think I should wear?"

I said, "Think of a summer garden. You see pink roses. There are many pretty blooms but you do not remember one individual rose. A bed of cornflowers. You do not pick out a single flower. But see one dark red peony, glowing like a ruby in its leaves, rich and like velvet, and you say, 'What a lovely bloom.' Next day, you go again to look at it."

"I do not wear red."

I waited. "Mama would not agree to red," she said.

I sighed and said then I would of course design a head-dress to wear with blue or pink.

"Wait here," she ordered. When she returned, it was in triumph. "Mama has said yes. One thing, if she believes I will outshine everyone else, even the yokels, it makes her amenable. Even here, she must shine. We are getting silks sent from London. Our dressmaker is here with Mama. She is a Frenchwoman, the sister of my governess. We have dismissed the governess but kept the dressmaker."

As if, I thought, they were baskets of apples or pears and you preferred one and sent the other back.

She told me when I might call again. When I did, I exclaimed with delight at the red silk she had chosen. Soft and dark as a rose in bloom, the folds changing to purple or to brown, stiff silk but one that would sway when she danced. It would make a perfect crinoline. Three deep folds would be like the petals of a rose. But the dress was not my concern, and I designed a head-dress made of two bands of silver ribbon which joined the roses I made from the silk and which framed her pretty face. She looked, I told myself, girl-woman. I think she knew it.

When she had tried on dress and head-dress she

nodded. This was our thanks, the Frenchwoman and I. But we did not need words. I think we each saluted one another as perfectionists in our trade!

On the evening of the party, I was summoned by Miss Rose Henriette to supervise, with the French dressmaker, her toilette. Rose Henriette Hatton was much chagrined that as yet she had no French maid of her own. She grumbled about it as we dressed her. Then, without a word of thanks, she left us. Without a word, the Frenchwoman left too and I stood there, uncertain what to do next. There was a knock at the door and Solomon Figg brought me a message from Miss Hatton. I was to partake of a light supper with her. Miss Fairclough had been fetched from the village and was here already.

"Miss Hatton is an angel of kindness," I said as I followed Solomon. He heard me and turned and nodded his head and his face split seemingly by a wide white smile. Miss Hatton was greatly successful at inspiring devotion.

We sat, Emmeline and I, and talked of the party below and Miss Hatton did not make the tactless mistake of saying what a pity it was girls like us were not dancing too. She talked of places she had visited when she was young, people she knew, and occasionally her astringent tongue described some of the ladies of Great Ezekiel. We could not help but laugh.

But all the time I listened and replied to her questions and smiled, while I ate and drank, I thought of him. He was below and he was dancing with his pick of pretty girls, as I had been told. This huge mansion was his home. One of his homes, I wryly remembered. When his father died he would be immensely rich. The family fortune was added to every day by golden tributaries from mill and mine, by trade, by coal and iron. His father and his stepmother accepted this flow of money with a coolness suggesting they took it for granted, they would indulge their own wishes, there were others to see to the job, as it were. And among the others was included Robert. Mr Hatton indulged his medieval fancies, there in the north. His wife travelled like a Queen around Europe, buying pictures and furniture, antiques, hangings and carpets, crystal and silver, gold and bronze, to furnish the house she occasionally stayed at. I wondered how long—a generation or two?—it would take for such people as the Hattons, having purchased this lovely country home, to be accepted as gentlefolk, born to the scene. Money turns the key with great ease, I thought. Rose Henriette's children and grandchildren will be gentry, no doubt about it. I hoped their manners would be an improvement on hers.

Julian and Emmeline and I, not long before, had discussed Robert, and did it with a kindness that went deep because we were all fond of him. Julian had concluded, with sadness, that Robert's present life was dictated by his deep sense of duty towards his parents. "I think he will be happy when he finds a woman to share his life," Julian had said. (I remembered his every word.) "When he has his own family, he will be working for their good, and it will be good for him. He works hard now, none harder, but I must say he gets little thanks for it. He is clever, as well as likeable. And he has a great asset in that he seems to be able to pick the right man for his position. I have not known him fail. This is why the estate here and the two in the north are so excellently run. Rob leaves his men to get on with it, and they are loyal to him, every one. But I believe he throws himself into work to forget so much. His father does not want him. His stepmother is an unhappy lady. When the boys died, she seemed to die herself. Oh, she is very fond of Rose Henriette but she adored the boys. I believe she guesses at the depth of Robert's compassion for her but it only makes her less sympathetic towards him. If he left, she would not miss him. But I wish he would leave, marry and leave, and cease being a shadow man."

I asked what life he thought would suit Mr Hatton. "A country manor," Julian said. "His own estate, for he genuinely loves the land. His home, though, would be overrun with people seeking him out. Not everyone would want help. There are many who greatly love him, I pray," Julian said, "he finds a wife, and soon, for then he would find happiness since she would be the only woman for him."

Tonight, I thought, he is very far from that country estate Julian dreams of for him. He is part of the scene below, he is its host, a scene as ostentatious as any London ball in the Season because a party such as this was Mrs Hatton's chance to show what perhaps she called 'the natives' just what money would buy. I had glimpsed the ballroom. Swags and swathes and vases and pots of sweet-scented roses. The candelabra with hundreds of candles to light the scene. The floor bright and polished as glass. Sofas in rich brocade around the room. I could only guess what dishes and what wine would be offered there.

I imagined, though I could not hear a note, the music of the waltz, the crinolines swaying, white shoul-

ders gleaming, pretty faces smiling. And mamas casting
their eyes towards Mr Hatton. Rose Henriette, like a
dark red rose, the centre of attention which was what
she wanted. Her mother in silk and jewels.

Then my thoughts were interrupted as the door
burst open and this same red rose ran in, kissed her
aunt, pirouetted round and looked at herself in the mirror.

"Oh, I am having such an evening," she told Miss
Hatton. "I know this is just a country hop—"

"Do not be absurd," her aunt said. "And do not use
such a silly word to describe what has cast the house
into a turmoil for two weeks and will be the talk of
Great Ezekiel for two or more years!" But these were
only words. She could not be cross with her niece who
tonight looked so pretty, so much in love with life.

"Why, the little milliners!" Rose Henriette said when
she spied us. Then, to me, "I have to thank you for
your idea. The red is a great success. I have been com-
plimented upon it all evening. When I am married, I
may give you and your shop my patronage."

Her aunt said drily she was sure Miss Bates would
pray for that day to come fast. Then, "Is Robert enjoying it?"

"Oh, duty dances," Rose Henriette said. "He is very
good about them. So is Julian. But Robert seeks out
the shy girls and the dowdy better than Julian. Julian
looks as if his mind is elsewhere. Anyway, he is cor-
nered at the moment by the archdeacon's wife."

I would not look at Emmeline. I heard Rose Henriette say, "Though Arabella is not dowdy nor shy and
Robert has danced three times with her. I am certain it
has put her into the seventh heaven of delight. You

know, Arabella might suit Robert," carelessly. "He does not need a rich wife and she is my friend. It would be cosy."

"Robert will choose his own wife," Miss Hatton said sternly.

"Well, he is taking too long about it," said his stepsister. "I am sure if Dick were alive, he would be married by now. Anyway, if I feel bored, I will try to push Robert and Arabella together. It serves well to have a sister-in-law one likes, and she and I laugh at the same people." Then she whirled out again. Miss Hatton said, "You need have no fears about the child pushing Robert into any girl's arms. He will choose when he is ready."

I would not even think of it, I told myself. It could not happen. Not Arabella.

That night in bed, when I held the little ivory angel to my cheek, I wept bitterly.

Twelve

There reigned in Great Ezekiel, socially, six ladies who went by the name of the Grand Inquisitors, a name they earned by the painful and often cruel scrutiny newcomers were subjected to by these ladies. They were questioned about birth, money, background. If they failed the test, then they were relegated to some outer circle where a cool nod was all the Inquisitors would allow when they met. Like cruel children, the six ladies were copied by other ladies who may have hoped that one day they would be Inquisitors too.

They were: Lady Dalrymple, the prime mover and the most cruel, Lady Gosling, Mrs Frobisher, Mrs Foster and Miss Smith-Brown and her sister Gladys. I think Lady Dalrymple would have liked to condescend to Mrs Hatton since the latter's vast fortune was derived from commerce and industry but even Lady Dalrymple was not stupid enough to 'cut' the Hattons.

If she had, I think the sycophants would not have followed. The Big House here was Windsor Castle, its invitations as greatly prized.

I had heard tales of engagements broken off because the young man in question did not equal so-and-so's daughter in rank. Mrs Foster's daughter was broken in spirit, followed her mother like a lap-dog, and, incensed because she believed the girl would never now marry, her mother did not let one opportunity pass without belittling her daughter and reducing her to tears, then calling her a cry-baby. The daughter was twenty-three years of age. I knew because I once tried to show her a bonnet, a pretty thing trimmed with cherries, and her mother snatched it out of my hand and laughed her loud bray. "My daughter is twenty-three, not sixteen. Do you want her to look a laughing-stock? She could never wear this. It is for pretty, lively girls."

I heard of young wives who wept because they were not invited to rout or dance or party. I heard of weddings solemnized with all the panoply of the church where each party loved someone else, not the partner with whom they walked out into the sunshine and the rose petals thrown.

Gossip was stored, polished and passed on over tea and macaroons. Poison was dropped into ears. Victims were marked out.

I hated all six of them but Emmeline was an angel of patience when petulantly they tried on and tossed away one bonnet after another. Having chosen, they haggled over the price. But Emmeline was prettily deferential so that I thought they could not help but like her. I was proved wrong.

At the end of October, Lady Dalrymple, for once overcoming her parsimony, for which she was noted, decided to give a *conversazione*. She implied, condescendingly, this was her answer to the Hattons' summer ball. A *conversazione,* I was told, was not as frivolous as a ball. Music. Light refreshments. A talk on Italian painting by a professor known to her ladyship. At the end of the evening, no doubt you fulsomely thanked Lady Dalrymple for an intellectual treat. You had better thank her.

While the village hummed with preparation for this event, Julian declared his love for Emmeline, proposed marriage, and was accepted. To me, in his happiness, his honest delight and love for my friend, he looked more boyishly handsome than before. And if love can add to natural beauty, Emmeline was radiant. "I always said you would marry a curate," I said, hugging and kissing her.

She told me that wherever she and Julian went, Jamie was to make his home with them. Mr Hatton said he would pay for the boy's education, and Julian said he himself could never leave the job unfinished and turn Jamie over to some other tutor. He said he would get Jamie into Oxford, of course he would. "But there is a black side, Martha," Emmeline said. "'Parting from you will be like tearing away the half of me."

I felt the same but I would not spoil the moment by showing it. I said, "I will visit you so often, you will get to sigh when you hear from me. 'Julian,' you will sigh, 'Martha asks if she may visit again—' "

"I will never say *again* and I will never sigh!" she cried. "Nor will Julian. He calls you a true and real person. Martha, when will you marry?"

"Now, do not get us both to the altar and the shop neatly shut on the same day," I parried.

"Martha?"

"Well?"

"You are not in love with—with—?" But at my uncompromising look she could not say the name. "Of course you are not," she said hurriedly. Then, "Though he is a charming and kind gentleman."

Julian gave Emmeline as a token ring a ruby set with pearls which had been his mother's. That sweet lady wrote from Yorkshire to say she had always longed for a daughter and could hardly wait to welcome Emmeline.

They were to go to Yorkshire on the Monday. Julian took morning service on Sunday. The news of the betrothal was all over the village and, I suppose, had run uphill via servants' talk to Great Ezekiel.

Heads turned when Emmeline and I entered the church. Her cheeks were pink. I felt as proud as a peacock just to sit beside her. After the service, we stood outside, as we usually did, to greet and be greeted by our friends and acquaintances. (We knew better than to greet the Inquisitors. A deferential deep curtsey was expected and that we gave.) I hoped Emmeline would receive some felicitations upon her engagement. It would make her so happy.

Julian stood, robed, outside the church door and greeted the parishioners and shook their hands. He greeted Lady Dalrymple and held out his hand. Her ladyship swept past like a galleon in her crinoline, the dewlaps on her face quivering with wrath, not giving him a glance. The other five Inquisitors did the same.

Julian said good morning to each of them. I could not look at him, he looked so angry.

But they had not finished. They saw Emmeline and they clustered together like a flock of crows and talked of it, loud enough for her and Julian to hear.

"I could scarce give it credence," said Lady Gosling, a tiny woman who looked like a withered rose. Her half-dead daughter stood beside her, staring at the ground. "When my maid told me, I could not believe it. The man is mad. His priest should speak to him. What hope has he of a parish with a working-class wife?"

"A cheap milliner," bleated Miss Smith-Brown. "No one will accept her or him. She will drag him to the depths."

"From the time she came, she set her cap at him," said Lady Gosling.

"You mean her bonnet," snickered Gladys Smith-Brown. She peeped at us to see how we took this.

"A man of God," boomed Lady Dalrymple, "and a common working girl."

"Come home," I implored Emmeline. "Before I forget that Dorcas worked hard to bring me up as a lady."

Julian was not long in joining us in our rooms behind the shop. It was Emmeline who tried to soothe and to calm him and me. It was we who raged while she remained cool and said the women were to be pitied. "If I thought there was any truth in what they say, I might worry. But I do not think so. My father and my grandfather were parsons—"

"It would not signify if they were navvies," Julian roared. "I am marrying you."

"And my mother was a doctor's daughter," Emmeline said. "More cake, my love?" to her betrothed.

"I shall leave this damned place," he said. "And it is damned while it spawns those women."

You are better than Mackays' theatre, I thought.

"Would Australia suit you?" he asked Emmeline who took his hand and held it and said, "If you were there."

I was glad when they left, the next day, for Yorkshire, for Julian, if he met one of the Inquisitors, would vent his anger on them, and Emmeline did not want this. That morning Lady Dalrymple honoured me with a visit to discuss a new bonnet for her *conversazione*. I was given to understand that bonnets would be worn at such a dignified and cultural gathering. Head-dresses, such as she had seen at the Hattons' ball, were too flippant. She did not use the word but it was what she meant.

Now that she wished me to do her a service, she was inclined to tolerate me. "Such an event is a great deal of trouble to organize and I am known for perfection in all things. I have not Mrs Hatton's army of sixty servants but my own loyal little band work hard. And they expect no extra remuneration."

I did not suppose they would get it.

"My drawing-room," she said, "will hold fifty."

I made a sound indicating I was impressed. Then I plunged into flattery waist-high. I said she was a lady who could wear something stylish in the latest manner. She stared complacently at her bloodhound looks in the mirror. "Perhaps," she agreed. "As a gel, I was run after." I sketched what I had in mind and showed her. I told her how it would look made up. I said it was the latest French model. I lied like a trooper. "Forgive me if I sound presumptuous," I said, "but for such an occasion, might you not wear something other than black?"

Before she could remind me that a lady always wore black, I said, "It is your evening, your ladyship, and you should be distinctive. You owe it to yourself." I told her what shade I thought she should wear. It took me fifteen minutes to get her to say yes. "One thing," she ordered me as she left, "I do not wish another soul to know about this. I wish it to be kept secret until the night of the party."

I said, and I meant it, that I would not breathe a word.

I thereafter interviewed, at intervals, and on their own, four of her friends. Miss Gladys Smith-Brown was away for a month. This made it easier for me. If she and her sister had both been going to the party, I might have found it risky. Each lady fussed, smiled, coquetted horribly and told me she wanted something quite unique and I was to keep it secret. I promised.

I stayed up very late each evening to make the bonnets. I told Jamie not to visit me. He said he would stay away and said he would tell Mr Hatton to stay away too. "He is at home again," Jamie said. "He asked me to find out if you needed anything. He said, 'Is she looking after herself? Is she eating well now that she is alone?' I told him I was sure you were eating well because you are fond of your food."

"And that rubs out any romantic notions he may have of me," I said, "as a pale, interesting girl." I threw an apple at him which he caught and ate.

I delivered the bonnets in the evening dark which

pleased my customers though not one of them offered me a hot drink, among the servants, after my trudge up the hill.

I wished I had been an invisible guest at that party in the drawing-room where fifty people could be gathered at a pinch. However many people, you would never hide five identical magenta bonnets. Each was an exact copy of the other, and not one of them flattered its wearer. Magenta velvet with magenta streamers. A fall of magenta feathers at one side, a cluster of wheat dyed magenta, at the other. A lace edging, snowy white, framing those sour, sallow faces. It was the ugliest bonnet I had ever made and I made five of them. When I had described it, and I swear I did describe it honestly, not one of the women had the taste to shudder, and every one, thinking she would stand out in it (as she did) grabbed greedily for it.

I wrote Emmeline a note, telling her I was leaving for good. I told her what I had done but not why I had done it. She would guess this, laugh a little, perhaps, but also weep for her impetuous friend who had waited, and not had to wait long, for the chance to avenge that hateful episode by the church. I knew it was not my 'place' to try to get even with these ladies, but for one glorious evening I had forgotten my 'place' and done what I wanted to do.

I supposed that in the stews of Seven Dials a virago would sail in and fight with her fists. I did it the only way I knew but I was finished as a milliner. I also knew this but considered it worth it, a hundred times.

Emmeline was due home the day after the party. I was sad to leave and did not travel towards London with the anticipation with which I had once gone. But there were times in the railway carriage when I had to bite my lips not to laugh and when I gained some curious looks from my fellow travellers because my shoulders shook when I thought of my five magenta bonnets.

Thirteen

I did not stay with Mrs Jarrett in London because I thought Emmeline would ask her first if she knew where I was. I journeyed to East Frobisher to look for Sarah Prendergast. I suppose in some way I was returning to the scene of my first years, and felt I might hide there.

Sarah, I found, was now Mrs William Drew. He was a prosperous farmer who had worn out two wives through child-bearing and hard work but now, in his fifties, let his eye light on Sarah and asked her to marry him. The shrewd woman knew there were daughters to look after the house, sons to see to the fields, and what William wanted was someone to look after him in his old age. In return, he doted on her. He gave her everything, from dresses to his attention and caresses, which he had never given his first wife and her successor. The farm parlour was filled with new furniture, almost stifling it, in mahogany and leather. The table was covered in a red plush cloth which matched the Turkey carpet. The walls were hung with pictures in heavy gilt frames. It looked what its owner was, newly prosperous. But I rejoiced for Sarah. The child from the orphanage deserved it because she had worked hard and honestly all her working life. Mrs Drew, in black skirt and black silk blouse with cameo brooch, talked much of Dorcas whom she would never forget. "You are bonny," she said. "But your aunt was a real lady."

"Bonny?" I repeated. "Where did you get that word?"

It seemed William was from north of the Border, originally. When I said I would like to stay, if this was convenient, I agonized over mentioning money, and Sarah knew I did and her black eyes laughed at me in a way I well remembered. She said I would be very welcome as their guest. William would be glad to entertain a friend of his wife's. But she said abruptly, "What are you running away from?"

"Sarah," I said, "if I tell you that, I must tell you the whole story, go back to the day I visited my uncle. But Sarah, may we sit in the kitchen? You are so grand in the parlour, it quite daunts me."

"I only wanted to show it off to you," she said, and rose and I followed her gladly to the farmhouse kitchen with its grand baking smells, its stone floor and rag rugs, its polished wooden furniture and scrubbed table, the ginger cat with her litter of kittens, and with little daylight filtering through because of the magnificent geraniums on the windowsill. Sarah sat in the rocking-chair and I opposite her. A ham baked in the oven for the evening meal. Her step-daughters entered and left. There seemed to be a good feeling between them. The cat tired of its family and stalked out of the door. And all this time Sarah listened until I came to the last episode of the five bonnets. She laughed until she choked. Sarah, I guessed, was always amused at something that went against arrogance. She wiped away tears of mirth and said, "Your sweet aunt would have been shocked. But in the privacy of her room I swear she would have smiled."

I stayed there a week. The days were long because Sarah would not let me help with the housework. I repaid her hospitality by making new bonnets for her and the girls. Being Sarah, she asked if I would make one for William's sister who, Sarah said, would never forgive her for being able to offer such a gift. When I had worked this out to my mental satisfaction I came to the conclusion there must be a running battle between the sisters-in-law.

I did not meet anyone I knew in the village and did not wish to.

One noon time, when I returned to the farm, Emmeline and Jamie were there. It was then I realized perhaps how much I had longed to be discovered, after all. Emmeline said she had gone first to Mrs Jarrett who knew nothing and to whom Emmeline must write at once to say I had been found. "She could not make up her mind if you had taken ship somewhere and been wrecked, her favourite theory," Jamie said, "or if you were on your way to the harem to be the sultan's favourite."

How well he looks, I thought, and how dear to me. Tall, fair, with an easy smile and a charm of manner which would one day make the ladies flock round him.

The child of actors, it had not taken Jamie Moore long to emulate the accents of Mr Hatton and Mr Emmett. His voice was clear and pleasant and warm. But he was still young enough to blush when teased! He said, "Oh, Martha, such a lark! I wish I could have been a footman with a tray when each lady entered to think herself exclusively the wearer of the magenta bonnet! You never said a word to me—"

"You are a chatterer. You might have told someone who might have told someone else—"

"Mr Hatton, you mean? They never mention it without guffaws," Jamie said. I almost reprimanded him for the use of this inelegant word but refrained.

But I had to say to Emmeline that I was sorry I had spoiled the shop for both of us. "I was consumed with such rage," I confessed, "I thought of nothing except what I did. Now, perhaps, when I think it over—"

"You have spoiled nothing," Emmeline told me. She said that if I did not return soon she might suffer from the effects of overwork. She said she had never been so busy and having to leave the shop to seek me had meant orders piling up! "Not that I would not have gone to the ends of the earth, my love, to find you." She went on: "There are ladies in the neighbourhood who, if they cannot openly applaud what you did, are not displeased and show it by buying a bonnet from us. They ask after you but are not surprised to find you gone. One lady said it is sensible to know when to run! But now, I beg you, come back with us."

"If you stay, I must stay too," Jamie said. "Those were Mr Hatton's commands. He said that wherever you were, I was to stay until things turned out for your good. So I shall ask Mr Drew for employment, and

wear a smock." Saying this, he smiled sunnily upon the
four Drew daughters, two of whom blushed. One threw
her apron over her face, and the last neither blushed
nor looked shy but gazed steadily back at Jamie. She
was the one he looked at longest. My word, I told myself, you are growing up! Aloud I said, "What you say
is blackmail."

"Yes," he said. "I think Mr Hatton hoped I would
use it."

I said I would go with them but I would act like Dr
Manette in his cell at the Bastille. I would stay in the
room at the back of the shop for I could not show my
face in the front. Then I said, "Emmeline, forgive me.
I have not enquired after Yorkshire."

She told me Yorkshire was a very beautiful county.
"Do not tease me," I commanded. "You know what I
mean."

Julian's parents had welcomed her as a daughter,
and she had loved them at first sight.

"They told her and Julian to hurry and put up the
banns," Jamie said.

Emmeline said they would not marry for some time.
But I think she looked wistful when she said it. "Julian
must find a teaching post. He will help in the parish at
Great Ezekiel when he is asked but he has decided to
be a schoolteacher." Emmeline at once invited Mr and
Mrs Drew to her wedding, whenever it was and wherever it was. Sarah said they would come and William,
who had just entered, promised his wife a new gown
for the occasion. Jamie and the fourth daughter smiled
at one another at this example of connubial happiness.

There was no kissing Sarah when I left. I thanked

her for her kindness and shook her hand. "I am always here," she said.

When we returned, I did what I said I would do, I stayed in the workroom and in the kitchen while Emmeline reigned over the front of the shop. We had been back two days when we had a visit from Madame Ferrier. Tall, thin, stylish in a velvet cloak and a bonnet to match trimmed with feathers, she swept in.

She gave Emmeline her cheek to kiss. Emmeline, the favourite child. "Lock the door," she ordered before she turned upon me.

First she explained how she knew what I had done. Robert Hatton had called on her in town and told her the story. "Before I got some garbled version from a client. But no version," Madame said, "however much embroidered, can in any way be worse than the truth." She told me I was a midge, a mite, less than the dust. She said I had disgraced the name milliner. I had disgraced her because she had trained me. For a full fifteen minutes she castigated me on my insolence, rudeness, arrogance and conceit. On my stupidity.

I wondered what she would have done if she had a friend, close as a sister, who had been shamed in public? Not, alas, use bonnets as a weapon. This I knew. But when she said she took much of the blame, I said, "You did nothing, ma'am——"

"I have failed to instil into you a proper reverence for the customer, the person who pays our prices," she said, "and so enables us to eat and drink and keep a roof over our heads! Their custom is what we live by and what we jealously guard, however we may think they behave. We do not make fools of them in public."

She would take no refreshment but said she was due

to visit Miss Hatton. I nearly said, "Give her my love, ma'am," but bit it back. Then Madame condescended to tell Emmeline she was pleased to hear of her betrothal to the Reverend Emmett. "I shall make your wedding bonnet," she said. "I shall make it myself."

As I watched her leave, I told myself that there went my future as a milliner. For the sake of her own reputation Madame would see to it I was not employed near her.

The next afternoon when Emmeline was out of doors, there was a rap at the front door. "I am not opening it," I called. "Miss Fairclough will return presently."

"I do not want a bonnet," Robert said. "But if you prefer, I will come to the back door."

Convention has gone to the wind, I thought, when I opened the back door to him. But then, convention did not stand a chance with this man. If he found it ridiculous, he laughed at it so that it shrank to nothingness.

I envied this ability of his but decided it must stem in great part from one's background. You could please yourself if you were rich and well educated and confident. If you were certain of your place in life.

There was the word once more that went like a thread through all we did and thought. *One's place.* You only stepped out of it, it seemed to me, if you could afford to buy yourself out of it like my uncle Bigby, that rich Hampstead dweller.

He had been riding, he said. The groom had taken the horse back. Yes, he would take a glass of sherry. In the workroom, I thought. Not as cosy as the kitchen but less plebeian.

"Why do you frown?" he said. I told him. He said,

"It does not matter where we drink sherry if we are friends. Does it?" And waited for my answer.

At the word "friends", I could only smile. When I looked up he was staring at me. He said, "You are more beautiful every time we meet."

"You are teasing, sir," I said happily. "Though I was called 'bonny' by Sarah Drew. I am culling compliments."

"Mine was not idle," he said. "You must know you are beautiful."

"Not," I said again. "Emmeline is beautiful. I suffer from red hair. It is a great trial to me. I could wish I were dark or fair. But not red."

"You are absurd," he said shortly. "Mr Rossetti paints models who have red hair. He likes them enough to paint them."

Well, we are not going to talk about Mr Rossetti, I thought firmly. I said, "I am thinking of emigrating to America."

The sherry spilled over from his glass as he put it down sharply on to the table top. He made to wipe off the stain with his handkerchief. "Leave it, sir," I said. "It is only the work top." And I took a duster and wiped it dry.

"Why America?" he asked.

"Oh," I said, "I dream of wide horizons as I sit here. It is not a large room and it is having an effect on me. When I—" I swallowed, started again. "When I—did what I did—"

"Five magenta bonnets," he prompted.

I nodded. "The gesture was idiotically large. Would you say, sir, it was akin to tilting at windmills?"

"With greater effect," he said. "I hear the ladies are

squabbling among themselves, you have shattered their nerves and confidence so much."

I could hardly say, "Good—" I looked down at my hands but I could not stop myself smiling. "You are a good friend, Martha," he said. "Would you do the same for me?"

"If you are in trouble," I said and I did not smile now but looked at him, at the grey eyes in that beloved face, and I hoped I sounded sincere, "and if I can do anything on your behalf, I will do it and damn the cost!"

I thought he would not stop laughing. I had not expected the word to come out but it did and of course I was not sorry now that it had happened.

"But you could not help me if you were in America," he said. "Perhaps I should go there too."

"Not you, sir," I said. "Your place is here, in the English countryside. A house in the country and a family. Manly little boys to teach to shoot and to ride. Pretty daughters." I could not mention his wife. We talked a little while longer, then he asked me to visit the Big House next day. His aunt wished for me. I said I would be delighted. He left and I stayed there, not lighting the candle, remembering every word he said, how he looked, until Emmeline came in. "Dreaming, my love?" she said, bringing the cold air in with her, looking rosy and pretty *and sane,* I thought. Because the thoughts I have, I told myself, are the thoughts of a mad woman. A person is mad to think always and only of the unattainable.

The first thing Miss Bertha said to me was how greatly she would have liked to see the five magenta bonnets trying to look inconspicuous in Lady Dalrymple's drawing-room. "I do not know how many minds stayed on the discourse on Italian painting," she said. "I hear there was more hilarity than there has ever been at Lady Dalrymple's. Her parties are not known for being jolly affairs. Five bonnets and they dare not wear them again. It is what I would like to think I would do in the circumstances."

I was certain she would do it but did not like to say so.

Then she said, "Be my companion, Martha. You have a talent I admire."

"For bonnet-making, ma'am?"

"For making me laugh. Sometimes, the days are tedious and the hours seem long. I am not always well. I should like you to be here. You are a tender child, as well as amusing. Saying that makes you seem like a fresh garden pea. Compassionate, too, but not mawkish. And very pretty. I like pretty girls. You and your friend Emmeline are delightful to watch and to listen to."

I could not remember when I had been praised as recently. Bonny, beautiful, pretty. They were being kind, I thought, for there were still times when I looked in the glass and studied my face I thought myself not much changed from Turnip Martha. My cheeks were pink, my eyes bright. I was glad I had such thick black lashes which I thought might in some way take the glance away from that shameful hair. But I was not a patch on Emmeline. It was she who glided, who had the softer voice, it was her shoulders that were smooth as marble to suit the current mode. Not that she ever showed her sloping shoulders in an evening gown. We did not possess such a thing. It was Emmeline who had the downcast glance, the swift pretty upward turn of the head.

"What are you thinking of?" Miss Bertha demanded.

I apologized and said I was thinking how pretty Emmeline was. She sighed and went on, "Well, do you accept? You cannot incarcerate yourself in your workroom for ever. It would take a brave young gentleman to seek you out there and fall in love."

Well, one sought me out, at least, I thought. I said, for I knew what she said was right, and I had gone too far to stay at the shop much longer, "Thank you, ma'am. You are an angel to me. When can I come?"

At which she laughed until she choked and I had to run for a glass of water and pat her hand and soothe her until she was normal. "That is what I like about you," she said. "You look romantic as Guinevere and you are as down-to-earth—"

"As a turnip," I agreed, also deciding I must read the Poet Laureate's "Guinevere" when I had the chance. Jamie would borrow it for me.

Miss Hatton rang for the housekeeper. Evidently she had been thinking it over before I said yes, and had everything planned. I was to sleep in the room next hers, and the room on the farther side was to be my sitting-room. I would take my meals with her when possible, otherwise in my own room. The housekeeper left to get ready what seemed to me a suite of rooms. Miss Hatton said she would pay me a hundred pounds a year.

"Oh, ma'am," I said, "that is too much—"

She looked at me and for once the eyes were sad, not mischievous. She said, "Save the money, child. I will not be here all that long a time. You will need it, later."

And when I looked at her I saw that the marks of illness and pain were deeper, that weariness was always there. I thought that I had taken so much from this lady, she had cheered me when I was sad, talked with me and guided me when my thoughts were in a tangled skein, helped and protected me. I bit back my grief and smiled my widest smile and said, "I shall be so happy here."

"Robert says you dazzle when you smile," she said. "Like sun on water. He is right."

But now I was not thinking of him. I was turning all my thoughts and all my strength on serving her.

Emmeline was pleased at what happened. I think that having me in the workroom was something of a liability if not a shame to her, and she would be easier in her mind on her own. She engaged a maid from the village, a young girl called Sophonisba Truly, to take out the bonnet boxes and to clean and dust the rooms. Each day, when I went for my walk which Miss Hatton insisted upon, I called at the shop (through the kitchen entrance) and picked up any bonnet Emmeline had laid aside. I would take it back with me and sew it in my room or when I sat with my employer who had given me permission to do this. Usually, she talked with her inimitable humour of the lady who had ordered the bonnet. But she was kind where it was the lady's due. It was only the pushing and the snobs that she castigated.

I settled in very easily. My duties were light for I did no housework. I fetched and carried and sewed for her.

I brushed her scant hair. I pressed and cleaned and aired her dresses and I made an inventory of her collection of bonnets. She enjoyed this. She had over a hundred bonnets. I nearly said once, "What will happen to them when you are dead, ma'am?" then, horrified, bit back the words. She said, as if I had spoken, "When I am dead, my clothes will be stored in the attics of this house. Have you seen the attics, Martha? They are enormous. One day, long after I am dead, someone will open the boxes. They will shake out my dresses and laugh at my bonnets. But perhaps they will give one of your bonnets to a museum."

I must admit it was a thought that had not entered my head.

At night, when I had retired but saw the light was still burning from the lamp in her room, I would go back and make tea and she would drink it and see that I fetched biscuits for myself. I would read to her, sometimes poetry, sometimes from the New Testament, until I saw her eyelids fall over her eyes, then I would put down my book and rise and draw the quilt gently over her shoulders and stoop and kiss her cheek. Sometimes she would lift a hand and stroke my cheek. I loved her very much. I always feel it is to my credit that I never once wept when I was with her nor showed how greatly I sorrowed for her. I think those who are sick have suffering enough without the burden of knowing they make others weep.

But in the morning she would tax her spirits and her strength again. I would dress her and she would lie propped on the sofa, talking, writing, laughing, reading to me from her work. "Will that go to a museum, ma'am?" I said.

"I might be grand and say my papers will be buried with me," she teased. "But Robert knows he is to burn them."

It was plain she was very fond of him. She told me she recognized his qualities and admired them. "But he is a lonely young man," she said. "He is not needed by his family. His father is in a world of his own. If he were a poor man he might be thought mad. Because he is rich, he is eccentric. As I am, I suppose? We waste our lives, having nothing to strive for. I wish Robert would ask the young woman he loves to be his wife."

The needle I was sewing with pricked my finger. I begged to be excused while I washed my hand in case the blood stained the white gauze I was fashioning for her. When I came back, I said calmly, "Your nephew is in love, ma'am, and would like to marry?"

"He says he loves her more than anyone in the world," she said. "He is not usually extravagant in his words."

Then why, in heaven's name, did she not put him out of his misery, I secretly raged, and make it easy for him to propose marriage? Surely she knew he loved her if he was as sincerely in love as his aunt said he was? Was she teasing him as we in the workroom in London knew minxes of fashionable society teased the young men who flocked round them?

"I hope," I heard her say, "everything will be resolved soon. Is that not how they write it in the romances, Martha? Do you not hope so, for his sake?"

"Yes, ma'am," I said, and my voice was steady. "Mr Hatton deserves a good and happy life. He has so much to give, himself, and does give, without stint."

"I shall tell him that," she said. "It may give him heart."

For the moment, I did not care about his heart. It was mine that broke.

Fourteen

At Easter the calm of the household was shattered by the advent of Mrs Hatton and Rose Henriette. I prayed my sister would not visit and my prayer was answered. Edith, one of the upper maids, told me that the friendship between Miss Bigby and Miss Hatton was at an end. Edith gossiped with me as I ironed Miss Hatton's gowns and steamed her bonnets. "You do those bonnets like washing and dressing a child for Sunday school," Edith said. She was a great one for criticism. But I tried to get on with the maids. I did not ask them to do one job which I thought was mine. I fetched and I carried up those endless stairs. And I was a favourite with Cook since the day I sought her out to tell her how much I enjoyed her cooking. "If you eat what Miss Hatton eats, you'll not satisfy a great girl like you," Cook told me. "Come into the kitchen whenever you like and fill up your empty corners." She may have done this herself because she was the largest woman I had ever seen and the finest cook in the county. If she had been otherwise, Mrs Hatton would not have employed her.

"I didn't care for Miss Bigby," I heard Edith say. "I reckoned she only aped her betters. I reckon she wasn't born to order others about. You can tell. The upper classes are wilful." (I admired the word.) "They will have you running and jumping through a hoop for them, all day. But you know they are used to it. You know that they think that is what you are here for and maybe it is. They don't see you as human. But that Miss Bigby did see you, though she pretended not to, and she enjoyed it which went to prove," said Edith, "she wasn't born to it. She couldn't carry it off. I'll wager her father made his money recently. Trade, I bet."

"Tea——" I said involuntarily. "And railway stock."

"Tea, is it?" Fortunately for me she did not ask how I knew. "Well, bound to be money in tea. So many drink it. Tea or gin, you can't go wrong."

"Why have they quarrelled?" I asked.

"What do you think? A man, of course. A man called Mr Comstock. Bevan Comstock. I think it is Miss Rose Henriette he is after but failing her, any heiress will do. The young ladies admire him no end," Edith said. "Somehow, it is a great thing to be seen in his company. I suppose," she went on, "a young lady would feel pleased if it ended by her being the one richest enough to buy him."

Edith's was a hard philosophy.

She said, before she left, "I suppose Miss Bigby's father would like to buy a gentleman for a son-in-law. To forget the tea."

Mr Hatton had mentioned Bevan Comstock. After this interlude with Edith, I took to noticing Rose Henriette, and it was my opinion that here was a girl mischief made even prettier. In the ordinary run of days, Rose Henriette, bored unless there was a party or a throng of admirers round her, would let her lips droop and her eyes glaze over. When she was planning something, be it party or intrigue, I told myself, she sparkled. I supposed that Mr Comstock, who was not in the district, wrote to her by some means. It surprised me that a girl as intelligent, because she was intelligent and well educated with a grasp of things when she took the trouble, could wish to live out the heroine of a foolish romance. Up to now, I supposed she had been denied little, and now she wanted Comstock, spurred to this by the knowledge that her best friend did too.

One day Robert talked to me again about him. Miss Hatton insisted that every afternoon, wet or fine, I took a walk in the grounds. The rain had stopped today and I walked to the top of a little hill and sat in the pretty marble folly there which had been fashioned like an Italian temple. Some days, when the sky was blue and the sun shone, it did not look out of place but on wet days I always thought it looked a sad sight as if it were homesick for Italy.

It had rained for some days and there were sheets of water on the lawn and water still dripped from the branches of the trees but where the light touched them and their new green leaves it seemed to sparkle. I love the start of a year, the spring. I think, "This year will surely improve on the last." Life, I thought now, had not been too cruel to me. People suffered worse things than being thrown out of their family. I had made wonderful friends. But I hoped that what was to come would not be too full of heartache. Translate that, I ordered myself. I did. I hoped that whatever happened to Robert, it would be for the best and that he would be happy with the woman he loved, and that wherever I was I would hear of it and rejoice for him. Of course I should hear. I would be told about him by Julian, and I would be happy for him. Then why did a tear steal down my cheek? Perhaps the promise of spring was for others, after all, and I knew that it was.

Then I looked up and he was walking towards me. Hastily I took out my handkerchief and wiped away the tears. If he noticed, he said nothing. He greeted me and stood leaning against one of the pillars looking down on the lawns and the trees and above the trees to where the river wound to the sea in the distance. "There is no country more beautiful than England," he said.

I agreed though I had to say I had not seen any other countries. He asked me if I wished to travel and I said I had not thought of it. It was all very stilted. The pause lengthened. Desperately I wondered what I might say but I wished him to speak first. After all, he was not Jamie whom I might interrupt and talk down and laugh with and tease. He came and sat beside me and said, "No bonnet talk today, Martha?"

"I bore you, sir, with my bonnet talk? I am certain I do. But it is what I live by, or did."

"God, no, you do not bore me," he said violently. If I waited for him to apologize, he did not. "Perhaps I have heard my sister say, once too often, 'the little milliner'. I feel I could take a hairbrush to her."

"Pray, no sir," I said, alarmed. "It is common coinage. *The little dressmaker. The little tailor. The little milliner.* And it is absurd because I am a tall girl. Five foot, ten inches. That and my red hair—" I said. "I consider I am unfairly burdened. I think they try, the people who say *the little milliner,* to add just one more, perhaps unnecessary, cubit to their social status. It makes them feel better than we are. As if you could not have a tailor six foot tall and gloriously handsome."

"And a milliner five foot, ten inches, and beautiful."

"There," I agreed. "You have made me feel better."

"And you are humouring me. There are three people," he said, "I find it easy to laugh with. You and Julian and Jamie. Jamie is becoming a rare young man—"

"A rare young devil," I said, but smiling. "I am so glad, sir, you gave him his chance." I shivered and he asked what was wrong and I said what Jamie had said, that if he stayed in London the city would devour him. "It is not fair," I said, "that children should suffer through no fault of theirs, that they are starved and destitute and exploited. People say they will get their reward in heaven but it seems to me they do not live long enough, some of them, to work hard at anything to merit reward! They say we are a great, rich country, growing richer. I do not consider a country rich which neglects the poor. We may have great characteristics but compassion is not high among them."

"Something has happened to you, Martha?" he probed, gently, but I collected myself. I smiled and said no more. So he said, "Do you have an especial dream for yourself? I think you do. That you marry and have a family and bring them up lovingly and— yes, merrily for that is another word for you. When you are happy, there is no one whose company I would rather be in. I have told you, you dazzle when you smile. You will have a happy family, no doubt at all."

I said abruptly, to put an end to these words which were turning a knife in my heart, "If you will forgive me, sir, I do not know how many times I must repeat that I do not intend nor wish to marry."

"You are not cut out to be a shopkeeper."

I blushed but agreed this did seem so. I said, "When Julian has his school, perhaps I might act housekeeper to Emmeline's headmaster's wife. Or keep house for Jamie. That should be fun enough. Until then, and I fear it may not be for much longer, I only wish to serve your aunt."

Then he said, "Will you help me? You said once that you would and damn the consequences."

I scolded that he should not remind me of this. "There are some things in my life I should prefer to forget." I thought for a moment then said with truth, "By heaven, they are mounting."

I think I loved him most of all when he laughed for then his face was as young as Jamie's.

But now I listened without interruption to what he had to say. He talked of Bevan Comstock and his chase after Rose Henriette which, after all, it was—a chase with a very rich heiress for prize. Mrs Hatton was leaving, next day, for Yorkshire but Rose Henriette stayed on. His father was not too well and had sent word he did not want his daughter near him since she was not of a particularly docile disposition. No, I thought, she is not. So Rose Henriette stayed on here, and her brother said he was suspicious of the obedience with which she had agreed to do so. Usually, she complained there was nothing here in the country but this time she urged her mother to journey to Yorkshire to her father to see to him. "Somehow," Robert said, "Comstock is in touch with her. I am certain of it. Someone acts as go-between. A maid, perhaps. I am not all that concerned about her but I should dearly like to know the truth. Martha, if you suspect something, will you tell me?"

I said thoughtfully I did not know what I should look for. An air of excitement when she was alone and believed she was not watched was not total evidence that a young lady planned her elopement. But I said I would do all I could, and I meant it. "If she is planning to elope," he said, and the word sounded so ridiculous we smiled at one another and I swear I felt at the moment a grown woman to Rose Henriette's child, "she will do it when her mother is not here. The only suspicion I have is her eagerness to get my step-mother to my father's bedside. If Rose needed her mother as chaperone for a visit or a ball, she would persuade her to stay."

Three days after Mrs Hatton went to Yorkshire, I went into Rose Henriette's room and found her, cheeks blazing pink, reading a note with a smile like a little cat rounding out those cheeks. The smile of a young lady who has received confirmation of what she dearly wants! When she turned and saw me standing there, she shouted, "Knock before you enter my room. You are a rude oaf." I did knock but, engrossed in her note, she had not heard. She threw me a bonnet she wished altered. Then Solomon Figg knocked and told her Miss Bertha desired her. I think, if she was fond of anyone, Rose Henriette liked Miss Bertha. She slipped the note beneath a large pin cushion on her dressing-table and ran out. I followed her and so did Solomon. He walked back to Miss Bertha's room but at the end of the passage I turned and hurried back to the bedroom. I read the note.

I know that what I did was reprehensible and wrong but had I not promised to do what I could for the one person who meant more to me than anyone in the world? He worried over Rose Henriette, he needed help. And I gave it as I had promised.

I found him in the library and told him what I had read.

Two nights later I drove with my companions through the streets of fashionable Mayfair until we came to a short street, a cul-de-sac of pretty Regency houses. You would need a great amount of money to live here, I thought, and wondered how the gentleman we had come to see could afford it.

I alighted on my own from the carriage and walked up the steps and rapped at the door. I told the footman who I was. He went to his master and returned immediately with him. Mr Comstock pushed past me and ran out into the dark evening. A white arm was extended through the open window of the carriage, the folds of the black velvet cloak falling back to reveal it. Mr Comstock gallantly kissed the lady's hand, opened the door of the carriage and tenderly helped her out. He took her up the steps and into the hall. I was close behind as a maid should be. But the third occupant of the carriage, whom Mr Comstock had not seen nor was meant to see, now jumped out and ran up the steps and was inside the house at the same time as the rest of us.

Mr Comstock only said one word. "Hatton—" but if words might kill there was venom enough there. His blue eyes slitted for the moment, then he stood by himself and faced the three of us. As I have said before, he was a quiet man, a quiet, pale-faced, composed man, with fair hair and blue eyes. Impeccably beautiful manners and a lovely speaking voice. I suppose, while he was relieving you of your fortune, he would do it with gentleness and sweet thought.

I had never seen a fortune hunter before. I stared at him with interest "What are you doing here?" he asked Robert.

"Not accompanying my sister on her elopement to you," Robert told him. Then, "All right, Jamie, you can take that cloak off now."

Jamie was delighted to do so. He undid the ribbons on the cloak and took off the gown beneath it. He wore beneath them his shirt and trousers. He grinned at me. It was a lark to Jamie but I had been nervous, all the way here. But it had gone off easily. Robert had taken command. The note from Mr Comstock told Rose Henriette to come to this house at nine in the evening when he would have made plans for them to leave that night for France. I was astonished to see how closely it kept to the lines of a romance, and I wondered if writers wrote from life or if life so often went by the book.

In his low and beautiful tones Mr Comstock enquired after the whereabouts of Miss Hatton.

"I employed an old-fashioned method," Robert said. "I locked her up. She will not be calling upon you now or at any time."

"That is up to her."

"But I would say that if you do marry, you and she, she receives not one penny of her inheritance. She inherits from her maternal grandfather who was both puritanical and shrewd with a nose for fortune hunters. He could not stand parasites, having worked hard to make his fortune. In his will, it says that if Rose Henriette makes what the family consider an ill-advised match, she does not receive a penny. Anyway, she does not inherit until she is twenty-five." He looked at Mr Comstock's face and smiled. "Did she not tell you this? Or did she hopefully and wrongfully tell you everything would be all right, that the family would not wish to be disgraced? No, she apparently in the eyes of others is well endowed but she has no money of her own. She inherits half a million pounds in four years' time. By then, I am certain you will be married to a girl who has access to her fortune already. I do not think you will wait for Rose Henriette. I do not advise you to or I shall horse-whip you tonight, if I believe you are even considering such a course. No, marry the next girl on the list," Robert said. "One thing I will do. I will pay your debts. I will give you five thousand pounds if you leave England now. It will be in Paris ready for you to pick up and start the Grand Tour."

"Your sister and I love each other."

"Then live in a cottage and prove it," Robert said cheerfully. "Perhaps, after ten years, when Rose has children round her skirt and has lost her looks, we may take pity on her and give her say, three hundred pounds a year. I am sick," he said forcefully, "of talking money. But I know I must with you."

"You are offensive. Your sister will hate you for this," said his listener. "She does not love you now but thinks you a canting hypocrite. From what I hear, you are not popular. There is about you an air of insufferable righteousness—"

The effect of this childishness was considerably spoiled by Jamie laughing aloud. I bit my lip. "Indeed," Robert said. "I am a prig. But then, she is my sister—"

"Half-sister. I have heard her say she is proud of being just a half-sister. She makes fun of you," Mr Comstock said, "for your old ways, for the fact that you take upon yourself the burdens you do, whether asked to take them or not. She says you are boring and a sermonizer, and she is right."

"And she, for all her worldly airs, is vulnerable," Robert told him. "Now, we are leaving. These young people are tired and have to get home. I will come with you while you write an undertaking not to see Rose again. Then, when I have it signed in my possession, I will see that the money is waiting for you in Paris."

So Jamie and I went to sit in the carriage. Jamie said to me, "You are soft-hearted, Martha. Why are you crying? Because that worm said what he did to Mr Hatton? It is all he could do. And you, Martha, are just as bad to weep over it for then you are taking it seriously."

He was right. I kissed him briefly, blew my nose and stopped my tears. "A worm, indeed," I said aloud. "I wonder who his next victim will be?" Then I felt a coldness at my heart. Please God, I begged, not my sister. Arabella had no one to save her from Comstock. On the contrary, my uncle and aunt would push her into the marriage, not that she herself would be reluctant. I found at this moment I did not hate Bella nor wish her punished for what she had done to me. There was no crime bad enough to be punished by marriage to that man, I decided.

We were silent on the way back. Jamie slept. I saw that Mr Hatton did not wish to talk so I pretended to sleep too but when I did glance at him he was awake, staring I think unseeingly at the dark shapes of the trees beneath the moon.

Jamie and I were standing close to him when he unlocked the door of Rose Henriette's room. I think we both had the thought that Robert might need protection. But it was not he she flew at but me. She hit me across the side of my face with a force to bring tears to my eyes. But I would not cry. I stood there, looking back at her. "It was you," she said and the low, hissed voice with which she spoke seemed worse than a scream. Even she had no wish to wake the servants. "You stole his letter. You told my brother about it. You are nothing but a dirty thief. I had always thought you came from the gutter. I will kill you with my own hands—" She lunged at me again but Robert held her tight and made her keep silent. "I asked Martha Bates to help me."

"A servant," she sneered. "A miserable slut—"

He ordered her to stop. I wanted to turn away but I could not. I looked at Jamie and what I saw almost unbalanced me into hysterics there on the spot for Jamie was looking at Rose Henriette as he might have looked at one of the actors on the stage at Mackays theatre. He was appraising her performance. This thought steadied me, after my first gulp of hysteria. For that is what it was. A performance. Rose Henriette Hatton might act as if her heart was broken, her young life over, but what was hurt was her pride at being treated like a wilful child. In years to come, I silently told her, you may not even wish to remember this episode. When you are married to a gentleman of means, when you have your great house in the country and your mansion in Park Lane, you will not even recollect Mr Comstock if his name comes up in conversation. You will say you never knew him. But tonight, you must act as you are acting It is your nature. "You will have a corker of a bruise on your cheek, tomorrow," Jamie told me.

"I wish I had knocked your teeth out," she snarled at me. "What have you said to Bevan?" she demanded. "What did you tell him?"

"I made him sign a paper he would not get in touch with you again. Then I have made arrangements to pay his debts. At least," Robert said tiredly, "I will give him the money. I cannot guarantee he will use it for that purpose. And you," he told her, "go to Yorkshire, tomorrow."

"*No.*"

"*Yes.* I shall write to mama to tell her—"

"*No.* She will treat me like a gaoler. She will not let me out of her sight. She will have me on a leading rein—"

He looked at me and I truly could not bear to see

the look on his face as he saw the swelling on my cheek. I wanted to say it was nothing but I dared not.

He said, "You should not have struck Miss Bates."

"To hell with her," said Rose Henriette. At least, this was honest. "I shall get even with you," she told me. "Do not think I cannot. I will send you back where you belong. In the stews." She scowled. "That odious Bella Bigby is in Italy, acting the part of a princess, wallowing in her dreadful father's money. She has set her sights on him—"

"Go to bed," Robert told her. "You have a long journey, tomorrow."

Her last words to me were, "Yes, I will get even with you. What you would like and are angling for is for this fool to set you up in a house in London where you could be his mistress. You have ingratiated yourself with my poor aunt who is in her dotage. You are eaten up with the thought that you are as good as we are. Well, I will show you. Bella was right. She said, that first day, she recognized what you are. A common toady. An ingratiating slut—"

I fled. Jamie told me later he left when Robert carried Rose Henriette to the chair, picked up her hairbrush on the way, set her over his knees and started beating her. He told Jamie to close the door quietly.

Fifteen

From that time on, Rose Henriette made things as difficult as she could for me. She gave me gowns to mend where the tears had obviously been made by her own hand. She flung bonnets my way to take them apart and remake them and when I did, she threw them into the fire as impossible to wear. But I suffered all this because I believed Miss Hatton needed me. Though the bright spirit was not totally quenched, she grew weaker every day. Where she had talked and laughed, she was mostly silent. But when I caught her eye she would smile. I will wait, I told myself, until you have no more need of me, then I will go.

I heard, one day, from my friend Edith, the maid, that Miss Arabella Bigby was engaged to Mr Bevan Comstock. "So Miss Rose Henriette lost," Edith said with a modicum of satisfaction.

I asked Miss Hatton if she could spare me for a

night so that I might go to London on business. She said yes.

Mrs Jarrett seemed delighted to see me and said she had dreamed of me, two nights ago, that I was lost in a shipwreck. Since almost every one of Mrs Jarrett's dreams embraced loss of life at sea, I did not take much notice.

The next day I went to the mansion in Hampstead on the chance I would see my sister. Luck was with me because my aunt and uncle were in Bath, taking the waters, and she was there with my aunt's companion for chaperone, a pale, dispirited-looking lady named Miss Smith. I had handed in, at the servants' entrance, a note requesting Arabella to see me. I said I did not wish to borrow money.

She and I faced each other in the huge but over-furnished drawing-room. She was very beautiful in a silk dress of a soft rose colour with lace at the neck and wrists. I thought that she had never been young, not Arabella. She might have pretended to childlike prettiness to get something she wanted from doting parents but beneath the smiles and the soft talk was a mind as cold and as calculating as a machine. And a cold heart too.

The stuffiness of the room oppressed me after the elegance of Mrs Hatton's house. There was a feeling that each piece of furniture had spawned one or two pieces more, that no space on the floral carpet was empty but it annoyed my aunt. Two huge jardinières in the shape of elephants. Three sofas, I could not count the chairs. Tables with their tops covered with bibelots and photographs in silver frames. I was sure that if one said one admired something, my uncle would tell you in an instant where it was bought and certainly how much it cost. The wallpaper was dark red with a darker design, and each oil painting, mostly still life, had wide gilt frames. Curtains of net and velvet completed the claustrophobic effect. I had heard that air, here on the Heath, was fresh and beneficial but I do not think my uncle could have benefited from it.

Arabella sat on a low chair upholstered in red to match the walls. I stood facing her. She did not ask me to sit. She said, "When you have finished looking round the room in your ill-bred way, what is it you want? I shall give you five minutes." That was when she dismissed Miss Smith. "My mother's companion," Arabella said as the lady left the room. Miss Smith gave me a nod. I smiled a greeting. Then she was gone and it was as if she had never been.

I told her at once I had heard she was engaged to Mr Comstock. She rose and went towards the bell-pull beside the fireplace. I was quicker and stood between her and it. "You will listen," I said. "Blood ties mean nothing to you and I wish to God they did not to me. But I have heard tales about this man."

"Servants' greasy gossip?" she asked. But she did not summon the footman. I thought this girl was more to be feared than Rose Henriette. The latter was hot-tempered but my sister would drive in the knife quite ruthlessly, and be glad she had rid herself of an encumbrance.

I heard her tell me that I looked like a servant. "An ingratiating look," she said. "You will soon follow it with the servant's slouch. The inclination of the head that becomes second nature. Smith has it to excess. It makes me shudder."

"Then shudder," I said. "I have come to you for our mother's sake—"

"Do not dare to speak to me like this."

"Dorcas was your aunt as well as mine. They loved one another—"

"I said five minutes," she told me and looked at the bell-pull. Then she said, "Did Rose Henriette send you?"

"No one sent me."

"Mr Comstock, of whom you know nothing, whom you have never seen nor would see except a glimpse from the servants' quarters, is a gentleman," she said softly. "He comes of a good family. He has been to good schools."

Fleetingly I remembered the glint in this gentleman's eye when Mr Hatton had mentioned that he would pay him for staying away from Rose Henriette.

"He told me," Arabella said, watching my face, "that he felt much as Lord Byron must have felt when pursued by Lady Caroline Lamb. But he is kinder than Byron. He said that though Rose Henriette was an encumbrance, he tried not to let her know it. In the end, though, he admits he fled to France to get away from her."

I give Arabella this, she did not ask how Rose Henriette had taken it. I do not think she cared how she had taken it. If she had ended like poor Lady Caroline, Arabella would only have laughed, felt no pity. She said, "By chance I met him when I was travelling. He asked me to marry him and I agreed. My parents are very pleased. We intend to live abroad in Lucerne."

"Your parents will live with you?" I murmured, ironically.

"No," she said. "They will see little of me when I am married." And will die for news of you, I thought. They will exist from letter to letter from you. But they will die soon because you are their life. When you go, they have nothing.

But to pay me out for coming here and for mentioning her future husband's name, she had one last thrust at me. "Do, if you consider yourself at all, stop your antics where Robert Hatton is concerned. It is very noticeable. It was the joke of the house party, particularly among the gentlemen. 'Hatton looks haunted,' they would say. 'The little milliner is in full cry!' Robert is always kind to the lower classes. He tries not to show what he really feels. And to girls who are plain and awkward and out of things. He seems driven, foolish man, to cheer them up."

"Is that why he danced three times with you at the ball?" I said and then I left.

There were no tears now when I went down the hill and made my way back to Mrs Jarrett's house I was older and wiser in what could happen among family.

Before I left Mrs Jarrett's I met the two girls who had taken our places there. Imagine my surprise when they told me that Madame had once said, in front of all the workroom, "There is no one here who can fashion a posy as Martha Bates did."

When I reached the Big House it was to learn that Miss Hatton had died in her sleep the night before. I rejoiced that death had come like a friend, holding out its hand and gently saying, "Come—" to one who had more than her share of pain. But I wept bitterly for the loss of a friend and mentor. "What will you do?" I asked Solomon Figg. He did not weep, this great man who towered above me. He did not need to weep. He would carry his grief around with him always until he died himself. He said he would stay here. Miss Hatton had said that he could. He would tend her grave. No one else would do this but he.

"You," Rose Henriette told me, "are to leave at once." She paid me my wages, saying her mother would not wish to be bothered by such a detail. When I asked if I might attend the funeral service, she said, "Not as one of the household."

Robert was out of the country and they did not know if he would be home in time for the funeral. Edith told me this. I was certain he would make every effort to be here.

While I was packing my belongings, for now I only wished to get out of this house as quickly as possible, Rose Henriette swept into my room. She said she had come to make certain I took away only such articles as were mine. Then she saw my little angel. "This is not yours. I remember, it is Robert's. Where did you filch it from?" But now the tables were turned. It was she who flinched away from me as I turned on her as she had done to me, the night we returned from Mr Comstock's. "Put that back," I breathed. "If not, I shall not be responsible for what I shall do to you."

"It belongs to Robert. You stole it."

"He gave it to me."

"I do not believe you." But she did not pursue the matter. She watched me put the angel away in my bag. "Poor fool," she said. "You and he." But I knew one thing, that if you stood up to her she would back down. She ordered me never to return to this house.

I went down to Emmeline but she understood I

would not be staying. Never again. I said, "If it were not that you and Mr Emmett are affianced, I would think I had done you a disservice, coming here."

"It is to you the hurt has been done," she said. "Yet, being you, you could do nothing but love him."

There, it was out, and I did not refute it.

"He is the best and the kindest gentleman," Emmeline said. "To him, people are not graded into classes according to what they possess. They are human beings and he treats them as such. Probably that is why he is a lonely man. There are not many who think like he does in this age. I have heard Julian say that one thing that makes Mr Hatton blaze with anger is the cruelty that comes from arrogance and fortune. Martha, love, do not weep."

She sat beside me and took my hand in hers and held it. "You are not alone, Martha. I have told you, and we mean it, that Julian and I want you to live with us. When we have our home, it will be yours. You are not to think you have no home. Selfishly we want you, not only because you will leave no stone unturned to help us, but Julian says no cloud is black enough but Martha's laughter kills it dead. But do not, I beg you, take a job as housekeeper with any other family, Martha."

When I asked why not, she said she would be so jealous of the people who employed me, it would do her immortal soul no good at all. So, between laughter and tears, between thinking of the future and reminiscing over the past, I stayed one night with Emmeline before leaving for London. I bade Jamie goodbye and was told that if ever I wished for him, I was to write. Nothing would stop him coming to me. "Work hard," I ordered. "Be a credit to your friends."

"You are not going to America," he told me. "So do not make farewell speeches."

I asked Emmeline and Julian when they intended to marry and they told me truthfully it would be when they had sufficient money to start their school. They looked so wistful, saying it, I wished I knew the magic formula Midas had used.

Emmeline asked me, when we were alone, if I wished anyone to know where I should be, and I said no, not yet, and I think she understood.

So I left Lesser Zeke on a glorious day in late May with the trees in leaf and the sky blue and the birds swooping in the hedgerows and wild flowers very like the posies I had fashioned for my bonnets for Madame Ferrier. We had seen this place first in Autumn. In January, we had come here to start our great venture. One year and four months from that January, I was leaving. But I felt as if I had lived a lifetime in those sixteen months. I had been happy and sad, I had been foolishly quixotic over the business of five magenta bonnets. I had watched over a lady who had been kindness itself to me as she neared death which she did with a braveness and a spirit I would never forget. And I knew what love was, and would love the same man for ever.

That is quite a tally, I told myself, and you do not look a day older than when you came here. Let us hope, I told myself with more severity, your good sense has matured.

I stayed with Mrs Jarrett where there was one small room always free for what she called transients. When

I asked her where she learned such an important-sounding word she told me Mr Dee told her of it. "Short-stayers," she said. "Those who can't get in anywhere else."

It seemed to describe me.

I had sufficient money to stay with her for a few weeks before looking for work. I knew better than to try at Madame Ferrier's. I am looking for a miracle, I told myself, something to point out where I should go and what I should do. I thought I was the kind of girl who would do this. Sarah Drew, Mrs Jarrett, Madame Ferrier, Emmeline. They would not rely on miracles. Martha Bates would, though. Not because she believed there was a divine dispensation for her alone but because, I chided Martha Bates, she did not have enough sound sense to chart out a course she could take. My mind could only, in this miserable time, see one face, hear one voice. I spent most days, for the weather was warm, in the parks where I watched the people stroll past, and smiled at children in the care of nurse or governess. I thought, of course I did, of what might have been had I been born of a different background, accepted by Mrs Hatton, a friend of her daughter's. But I told myself, when I woke up from the dream, that these thoughts belonged to this time I was taking off from the real world. Perhaps, later, I would not dream about it again. But who could blame me now, with the chestnut trees in flower, the may and the syringa? It was the time to romanticize.

I was giving myself until the end of the second week for this holiday from reality. Then I received a letter from Mr Redding, the solicitor, asking me to call, and

again he had good news for me. Miss Bertha had left
me a house at the seaside resort near Great Ezekiel.

"Good property, very," Mr Redding said. He was as
breezy as ever but in the time since we had last met,
his hair had receded somewhat and his cheeks pinked
towards the florid. But he beamed at me. "Fancy yourself keeping a boarding house, Miss Bates, what? Make
good money in summer. Favourite place for middle-
class families. Or looking after the old ladies and gents,
eh? Ladies, alas, getting on in years, old gents finished
with their service in India and the East, looking for a
comfortable home. Yes, nice place," he beamed. I said
I knew this. I had lived near there. I dared not say too
much, my heart was too full. She had remembered me.
She was making certain I would not be destitute, her
stubborn Martha. I pressed my lips tightly together so
as not to weep while my heart silently said thank you
to her.

"Of course," I heard him say. "Companion, weren't
you, to Rob Hatton's old aunt? Lovely little lady. She
gave me a whacking tip every time I went back to
school. My own parents were in India and she said it
took a long time for a tip to come from there."

I wanted very much to enquire after his friend, but I
said nothing except that I would go and see the
property as soon as possible. "That's the idea," he told
me, cheerfully. "Whatever you decide, come and have
a chat. When your name comes up, 'pon my word,
Miss Bates, I feel ten times the man. Something
pleasant, each time, what?"

"Well," said Mrs Jarrett, when I told her, "I must
say people take to you, Martha. Property. At the
seaside." Her eyes rolled in her head at the thought.

But when I asked her to accompany me to inspect it, she regretfully refused. "The sea," she explained. "I only have to look at it and I'm no good for the day. It makes me weep so hard, thinking of all those lovely people drowned and at the bottom!"

So I went myself to the seaside town where once Emmeline and Julian and Jamie and I had visited, and Jamie had wondered if the others were in love, and had been relieved to hear of Emmeline's antecedents. I am close to you, my love, I silently told Emmeline, but I will not visit, not now. I have a great deal to think about.

I stayed at a boarding house of impeccable respectability, filled, it seemed to me, with the full-bosomed relicts of well-off husbands, for truthfully there was not a thin lady among them. The food here must be excellent. A few widowers, and I thought these the more helpless. They looked timid. Perhaps it was because they harboured the suspicion the widows eyed them as a fisherman his prey. Most of the ladies looked as if they would not be put down by Lady Dalrymple. No, I could not run a boarding house for ladies like these.

Next day I sat on a seat on the promenade, and half turned so that I was not facing the sparkling blue sea but looking at my property, the end house of some twelve facing the beach. A desirable position and a very desirable house. A small garden in front, steps leading to the front door, two large windows each side of this, five windows above, and above these the servants' attics. Mr Redding had said the former occupant was a wealthy East Indies merchant who had come home to find a wife and retire here but had died very soon. When he died, Miss Hatton, in Mr Redding's

words, snapped at it. "I think she meant it for you,
Miss Bates. It only came on the market eight weeks
back."

The outside was painted cream, the woodwork
around the windows white. The door was stout oak and
the brass knocker, when polished, would blink like an
eye in the sun, I thought. It was a truly wonderful gift,
and as it was meant to, it made the feeling of insecurity
fade. Insecurity and the fear it spawns, of accident, of
losing her employment, of illness, is the ghost which
haunts a woman working in London. Miss Bertha
could never have known what it was to be insecure but
this did not prevent her feeling for me. But I knew
that, for all this house I could hardly see now for tears,
I would willingly go back to the Martha Bates who had
gone that day to Mount Street and found, for the first
time, the generous friendship of Miss Hatton, I would
return to that poor and certainly none too secure girl,
to have Miss Bertha alive.

"I wondered when you would come," Robert said.
"Redding did not know the day. So I have waited for
you for two days which have seemed a lifetime." He
sat beside me and lifted my hand to his lips. "She
would not have wished you to sit here weeping.
'Robert,' she would have said, 'find the gel and comfort
her.' I have found you, Martha. And it is what I am
here for. To comfort you."

Sixteen

He did not ask why I was not at his aunt's funeral and I was glad. He told me he had returned with an hour to spare. I was glad of this too. And I asked not a word after his family for truly I was not interested in them. The family for me were just two people. I told him it was very kind of his aunt to give me this house.

"She was fond of you," he said.

I said, not above a whisper, "You must not say things to me, seemingly, that are too tender. I weep easily, these days. I think, now that I have not your aunt to look after, I feel unwanted. Do not breathe this to Emmeline. I know she wants me and would have me with her for ever. But she has Mr Emmett. Jamie has his own life to live. I feel unwanted," I confessed, "and the feeling is death to me. As though I have died, myself. I feel rejected of people."

"As your uncle rejected you?" he asked.

There was silence then, broken only by the cries of children, drifts of talk as people passed, seagulls screaming above the water. I watched a small boy bowl a hoop while his older sister followed sedately with her pet dog on a leash, acting the young lady, conversing in French with her governess. But the boy tripped and let off a wail of grief. The dog barked, the little girl ran and comforted her brother, in English this time. She gave him her handkerchief and ordered him to blow his nose. "You always run where you should walk," she said. Did this apply to me too?

All this I thought about because I found I did not want to think about what Mr Hatton had just said.

"The second time I saw her, I heard of it from Sarah Drew." I looked at him then and it was not the face I knew. It was dark with anger. He said, "I did not know you had family and said so but Sarah told me the story she had heard from you. She said you would not marry, you said, because of the treatment meted out to you by your own family, that you could not trust anyone. Is this true, Martha?"

"Except for Dorcas," I said, "I have no family. But why did you visit Sarah?"

He confessed simply, "I was hungry to know about you. I bared the bones of anything Jamie knew. I asked Julian what Emmeline said. It was never enough. So I visited Sarah Drew." Then he said what I knew he would say. *"Bigby.* I never connected the names. Dorcas Bigby and my sister's friend Arabella. Martha, your own sister, staying at the house, visiting the shop—"

"It is over now," I said. "And my sister's name will soon be Comstock."

He said he had heard of this. But one thing stayed in my mind. I had to ask. "Why did you go *first* to Sarah?"

He hesitated, then explained. "My aunt, as you know, admired fairy tales. I think she wanted to live one. She asked me how I could get you to the village, into the little shop you so admired. We both knew you would not accept our gift. So I went to East Frobisher and met Sarah who told me about your aunt—"

"The legacy," I whispered. "The one hundred pounds. It was Miss Bertha? There was no Toby Vole—"

"Do not sound so disappointed," he told me. "Your aunt must have had many admirers. I know Bertha would have confessed to you very soon. She was talking about it the last time I saw her. She wanted to know if I thought you would forgive her."

"Forgive her? It is the kindest thing I have heard of. And the name is perfect. Toby Vole. It was your aunt, sir, who thought this up?"

"No," he said. "It was Sarah."

I shook my head and admitted that if we both lived to be a hundred, Sarah Drew would never cease to astonish me.

"My aunt so wanted you near her," he said. "In any woman less loving and lovable, she would have seemed indulged. But what she wanted usually turned out for good. I wanted you there too," he said calmly. "And she usually tried to give me what I wanted."

I had no answer to this so was silent. Then he said, "Shall we inspect the property?"

We crossed the road and stood on the pavement looking at the handsome house. This is what I said.

"Indeed, it is a handsome piece. I cannot believe it is mine. Do you suppose Emmeline and Julian will marry soon?"

He did not look surprised at my mind jumping about thus. He said, "Very soon. Bertha left Julian a handsome legacy. She liked him too. She has left Emmeline some very good pieces of furniture to furnish most rooms in their new home. She enjoyed helping young people," he said. "It vexed her that only I was proving stubborn."

"Stubborn, sir?" I asked, surprised.

"She could not clearly see how I too might get my heart's desire," he told me, calmly.

I remembered the lady he was to marry and I did not answer. He sighed and said, half to himself, "Neither do I see it too clearly, not even now. But to revert to Emmeline and Julian, they are only looking for the right place for their school."

"Then they have found it. They may rent this house from me."

"And you would like the rent to be a peppercorn?" he teased. I told him I feared they would not accept the house as a wedding gift which was what I should prefer.

The house was empty of carpets and curtains and any kind of furniture. The sunlight poured in through the bare glass and filled the place with golden light so that I wondered why we bothered to choke the glass with curtains. "With Emmeline mothering the pupils, Julian teaching, Jamie as head boy, all that bracing air outside," I said, "if I had sons ready for school, I might send them here."

"I went to school at eight years," he said. This made

me reconsider what I had just thought. Eight years! Still, Emmeline would be kind.

We examined the kitchens, went up to the attics. Everything was as if made for what I had in mind. "You will persuade them to accept, sir?" I asked. "Silly pride may make them hesitate."

He said coolly, "I will tell them if I have time. But I have my own affairs to see to which are of more importance to me."

The red stained my cheeks. Up to now he had been so kind a companion, perhaps I had mistaken this for friendship, for a closeness of thought between us. I had presumed too much upon him. I stammered my apology and turned to go. "Sit down," he ordered me. "I am tired of chasing after you. There is no one here. In Mount Street, the day you thought I had designs upon you, there were servants within call. Here, no one. *So sit down*. And listen to me."

I whispered I could not see anywhere to sit. He led me to the window-seat, wiped it with an immaculate handkerchief, and sat me there, then sat next me. But I was silent for so long he had to ask what I was thinking of.

"Of Mount Street and that first day," I said. "I was a fledgeling. But so happy to be in the city. So enjoying Madame's establishment. Oh, she was kind to me. I remember it was a February day, grey, viperish with cold. My nose may have been red as a cherry—"

"Your nose is exquisite."

"I was so happy, though, the cold, the grime, being poor did not seem to count. There was that in me that saw only the best and the happiest."

"Now you are less happy?"

"Things are no longer black and white, good and bad. I am older," I said.

"Yes," he murmured. "You are all of twenty-two years. But you would still laugh on a viperish day in February, you know you would." .

"I have packed a great deal into life," I said with dignity, "since that day."

When he stopped laughing, I was smiling too. Then I sighed and said, "Sometimes a phrase pops out that is not ladylike. Dorcas chided me for it. She told me my tongue ran away with me and that all I did was laugh at it!"

He asked me if I thought Dorcas would approve of him. I tried to think what she would have said and came out with, "She would consider you a true gentleman."

"Then marry me, Martha." He said I looked beautiful even with my mouth open in astonishment. "But why are you surprised? You must know I love you."

"Indeed, I do not." I could hardly frame the words for shook. Then I rallied and said, "You mean to marry another lady."

"Do I?" He looked surprised, now. "Do you know who she is?"

"Your aunt told me you were in love with her. I said I hoped you would have a happy life, that you deserved it."

"That is what Aunt Bertha told me. But I think, much as we both loved her, she would grow impatient at us quoting what she said and would want us to use our own words. I may not have a chance to talk to you like this again. You have a way of disappearing and the days when I search for you and wait for you are like years. *There is no other lady*. My aunt meant you though she could not tell you so. She would have liked to, she loved her fingers to be in many pies, but this she could not do. I love you. Will you be my wife?"

"I have said I will not marry—"

"Do not punish me for what your uncle did," he said with a flash of anger and he was right, I knew he was. But I had been so long hurt by my own family, I could not forget it in an instant. He knew this and took my hands and held them and made me look at him. "Our marriage may not have been made in heaven, as they say," he said. "But it was made of my admiration for a brave, happy, beautiful girl with red hair—"

I sighed.

"And a laugh that warms my heart to hear it," he said. "A girl with compassion and a bravery to take on and rout five formidable ladies for the sake of her friend."

I sighed again.

"A girl my aunt loved. She had one grief, that she did not know, before she died, we would marry. But she said you would say yes. She also said, and she was right, you have no idea of your worth. She said, 'A girl in a million, Rob. So marry her.'" Then he said, "I am so tired of living other people's lives in other people's homes. I want my own life and my own family."

"But we cannot marry," I said though I was beginning to feel as though I was fighting a tidal wave. "King Cophetua—" I said faintly.

"If you did not weaken my resolve by making me laugh, I swear I would beat acceptance out of you," he said. "What about King Cophetua? He took the girl." He stared at me. "Pearls—" he said half to himself.

"Pearls, sir?" I echoed. He told me a lady with red hair who wore emeralds looked banal. "Pearls are your jewel. They have a sheen and a warmth. Oh, Martha, let me buy you jewels," he said with impatience. "We shall do good with my money. I have schemes and with you I can bring them about. There is great unfairness everywhere and I shall try to do what I can to lessen it. But I can be frivolous, surely? I can wish my wife to be the most beautiful woman? We shall dance, at times, listen to music, walk in the country. We will work all the better for this. I do not wish you to be a walking advertisement of what I am worth, as so many men wish for their wives. I do not wish to see you a doll, fashionably dressed. But I do want to make your loveliness shine, if not before men, then before me. Do not grudge me this. No one," he said half to himself, "has ever wanted what I had to offer except perhaps Bertha."

I said nothing, and he said, "So you are bound by convention, after all? Not the free spirit you seem? A milliner and the rich Mr Hatton, you think, cannot marry."

"I would not wish to say yes because you provoked me into saying it," I told him. "And that is what you are doing. I only know I have loved you since you met me filching sweets. Heavens, what an introduction. Oh, sir—"

"That is another thing. My name is Robert."

Then, of course, I could not say it.

"Try," he teased. "You cannot have called me Mr *Hatton,* in your mind, all this time. If so, you are polite beyond belief! Take the plunge."

I did and he kissed me.

The next minute I was down from clouds of glory to thorns around my feet. "What will your parents say?" But in his shrug, in the coldness that came instantly into his face, was all the estrangement he suffered. I will make it up to you, I vowed. Perhaps it is the truth that we do indeed need one another.

He said he thought his mother would only take to a daughter-in-law somewhere in the vicinity of someone's blood royal. "If we get a son, my father might like to kidnap him and take him north to try to pull Excalibur out of the stone!"

Perhaps, I thought, we shall have many sons and spare one for that lonely man in Yorkshire. I said, "Your sister?"

He grinned and agreed that Rose Henriette would not care for it. "Well," with a touch of arrogance, "we have disposed of them, of my family. Now, will you marry me, Martha?"

I said I should be honoured, adding, "And I will do my best to put up with your family."

His shout of laughter echoed round the empty room.

Seventeen

Today is my wedding day.

We are to be married in a small London church, no pomp or circumstance. Robert's family will not attend but my small circle of friends have said they will. Emmeline is in London with me. We are staying with Mrs Jarrett. "You," she told me, "marrying where you are marrying, to stay in a house like this! You could be at the palace—at one of the best hotels." "And you," I told her, "stop such talk or you will make me angry with you for the first time. This is my London home until I leave." She beamed at me.

Julian and Jamie are coming up from the country, and Sarah from East Frobisher. "If you see all this, Aunt Dorcas," I mentally addressed her, "I hope you are pleased. I am a very fortunate girl."

Emmeline and Julian made no stupid fuss about my offer of the house. I know they preferred to rent it.

They said so. Julian said, "I thank you, dear Martha, from my heart." Emmeline kissed me and laid her cheek against mine. Jamie said, "Put your sons down now, Martha, for the school." "You do it credit," I offered, and he said, "Yes, ma'am," with that smile of his which soon now will cut swathes in young ladies' feelings. Emmeline was to marry at Christmas; the school would open in the New Year.

It is a soft languorous September day, my wedding day. A day you would think was still summer until you saw the leaves were yellowing.

My gown, which Emmeline and I made, is cream silk, full falling from a tiny waist, roses woven into the silk. The silk is a gift from Robert as are the pearl ear-rings I wear with it, and the necklace. I am very tempted to move my head more than is necessary, wearing the drop ear-rings, to feel them swing. I have never owned ear-rings before.

When I tried on my wedding clothes, when we had searched but could find no flaw, nothing that needed alteration, Emmeline and I sighed at each other. We did not say a word. My bonnet was cream silk with a froth of orange blossom beneath the brim, framing my face. I do not know about museums, as Miss Bertha had talked of once, mentioning her bonnets, but I would never part with mine. Never. I was a bonnet-maker and only I could say what hopes and prayers, as well as all my skill, had gone into my wedding bonnet.

And the family? Robert's family? His mother hoped I did not wish her to present me at the London Season. When her son said no, she said she was relieved to hear it. His father demanded to know what sort of seat I had on a horse. When told I did not ride, he never said another word about the wedding. Rose Henriette had hysterics and told her brother she would be the laughing-stock of her friends. "They will ask me, whenever they see me, if my sister-in-law did not make my bonnet!"

Our little shop in Lesser Zeke, Emmeline said, was the haunt of ladies asking if the news was true, that Mr Hatton was marrying the milliner.

I did not care. We had decided to live out of the villages. There was a house Robert said he might buy, not large, he said, but quite perfect. A small park. From here he could still manage the great estate that went with the Big House. Silently I thought he would never be free of his family. When they wanted him, and it seemed they would always want him, he would be there. But not on your own now, my love, I thought. Whatever you wish to do, you must do, but I shall be with you. If I can, every journey you make, I shall make. *Patient Griselda,* they will say, giving the word its true meaning, but I shall not care what they say. When the babies come, that will be another matter. Anyway, I did not think their father would wish to stay long from them.

Sarah Drew had sent to me the tray and the teapot and the 'company' cups she had faithfully kept. At least, I was not going completely empty-handed into wedlock.

When I was dressed and ready to leave for the church, Sarah told me my aunt would be proud of me, this day. She had spent the night at the same hotel I stayed at when first I came to London. Tonight, she would be back in East Frobisher. Will, she said, would be depressed if she stayed too long. I could believe it.

He had paid for her to have made a handsome black dress for the occasion. Mrs Jarrett too, wore black. Emmeline's dress and bonnet were a soft misty blue. There were blue feathers at the side of her bonnet, dyed the same blue. I thought how elegant and stylish Emmeline always looked. It was inborn. Julian was fortunate. I suppose he knew.

Mr Dee was to walk with me up the aisle, in the absence of family. He had the day off from the office. Mr Diss was on holiday. Mr Dee was filled with self-importance. "A very rich family, the Hattons," he had told me. "Oh, exceedingly rich."

"The Midas touch," I murmured, remembering she who had once said it, sitting up in bed, bonneted in one of my bonnets far too sprightly for her years. I blinked hard. I must not weep now. She would have been angry with me.

"You may say that," breathed Mr Dee. "Indeed, the Midas touch."

And much good it does them, I thought, as much as to King Midas.

We arrived at the church to be met by Julian who looked worried and said Robert was not yet there. So Mr Dee and I, Mrs Jarrett and Emmeline sat in the cab and waited. Sarah went into the church. So did Julian and Jamie.

Then I saw a familiar figure approach. Tall, handsome, and so very stylish in the latest fashion it could only be Madame Ferrier.

I got out of the carriage. I was beginning to feel a heaviness of dread within me and perhaps, I thought, I would feel better in the air. Mr Dee remained in the carriage. Mrs Jarrett and Emmeline, as if to give support, stood one each side of me. Madame bent and put her cool cheek on mine. She said, "I could not let you marry, Martha, without being here to see it and to wish you joy."

I thanked her. She swept into the church. I waited for a little while until Emmeline said, not meaning it, she would prefer to sit in the carriage again, so we did.

We waited an hour and still he did not come. It was Mr Dee's turn to walk up and down outside the church. He would walk to the end of the road, peer in each direction, walk back, pass to the other end, and peer there. He is trying to conjure Robert to come, I thought.

I took my little ivory angel out of my bag and held it in my hands. I did not make the mistake of thinking it a charm which would charm him here. But it still comforted me.

First I had felt terror. Now it was a dead acceptance.

Of course it had been a dream and I had played the part of a silly romantic girl. The family had prevailed on Robert to think it over and admit it was a mistake. A man such as he could not marry a girl like me. I was common, a working girl. I would not know how to act in the great houses, how to conduct myself in company. I should be a liability upon him. He should marry an heiress to some great estate. With her acres and the Hatton fortune, their sons and daughters would be part of the aristocracy of this rich land. No, King Cophetua did not take this beggar maid.

Mrs Jarrett held my hand. She did not say a word, for she was a sensitive woman. Emmeline, when I caught her eyes, smiled the usual warm loving smile.

The bell struck the quarter hour.

I felt now as though Martha Bates was dying and that another girl stepped, phoenix-like, from the ashes, a girl who would leave the country, dye her shameful hair, beg her friends to say she was dead. But wherever I went, whatever I did, I knew that I should love him until the day I died, and after death throughout eternity.

I wondered, as one does, what sin I had committed to be thus punished? Pride, was it, in thinking he would marry me and I should make him happy as he deserved to be happy?

Then the second carriage arrived and he jumped out and ran to us and pulled me out and there on the pavement held me to him and kissed me. I do not think my friends were scandalized, not even the conventional Mr Dee. He probably thought that some urgent matter of business had held up Mr Hatton.

"Forgive me, my love. Please forgive me. I could not get a message to you—"

All I could whisper was, "It is quite all right—" as if someone had trodden on my toe in the waltz. I did not tell him, and I never told him, the base thoughts that had gone through my mind. When I remembered them, I was ashamed.

He said, "There, in the carriage, is the explanation." I peeped in to see the eyes of Rose Henriette glaring at me in fury. She could not greet me because there was a silken scarf tied round her mouth. Two more scarves bound her ankles and wrists. "I could do nothing but bring her with me," I heard Robert say. "Today, I dare not let her out of my sight. She is determined to wreck this wedding and I know she will not. She left a note in Mount Street to say she was running off with some man. She thought to ruin the wedding by making me spend time looking for her."

"Indeed, it would not have been the same without you," I agreed, and he laughed and kissed me again. Rose Henriette mumbled behind her gag. Julian, who had joined us, looked anxious. "You must come into church, Rob. The vicar is patient but he has an alderman's funeral after this—"

"The alderman will wait," said Mr Hatton with the flash of imperiousness I loved. "She—" pointing to his sister—"was two doors away, after all. A friend sheltered her and no doubt they thought it a great lark. One of the servants guessed and I hauled Rose out. She kicked and screamed all the way down the steps but she could hardly accuse me of abducting her since I am her brother. I shall have sore shins for some time where she kicked me." Then he said, and sounded young now and uncertain, "But now I don't know what to do with her."

Madame Ferrier, who had joined us, said, "Let her come into the church. I am certain Miss Hatton will not wish to miss the ceremony, now she is here." She stepped into the carriage and solicitously undid the gag.

"I shall be the laughing-stock of London," Rose Henriette shouted. "I know I shall. My parents are insane to agree. She will bring him down within a year—"

"Good enough for Mackays," I heard Jamie say, admiringly. I looked at him and he winked back at me.

"Miss Hatton," Madame said, "I think you should compose yourself, tidy your dress. I have a shawl you may borrow to cover your hair."

"I will go in there and stand up and stop the ceremony—"

"*Jane Eyre*—" Jamie said, delightedly, and clapped his knee.

"You must not make yourself look foolish," Madame told Rose Henriette. She went on, cool as a brook in winter, "I do not know how it happens, but the girls I employ are adept at picking up gossip. They are worthy of Scotland Yard in the way they hear of clues to a person's behaviour in such and such a place at such and such a time. They know a society story before it is half done! They know who has run away with whom, who is marrying an heiress because of his debts. By the way, Miss Hatton, did you know your friend, Miss Bigby, married Mr Comstock yesterday? I sent her the bonnet she ordered from me. I was pleased she remembered my establishment. But I should not be surprised if, by tonight, it will be all over the workshop that you acted as you did—"

"Trying to stop my fool of a brother from marrying a common milliner—" shouted Rose Henriette.

She should not have used the word. Madame did not change her tone but she said, "They will snigger over your behaviour which will, I am certain, not please you." And the word "snigger" wiped out the word "common". "Laughter," Madame said, "runs round London society quicker than a heath fire."

"They will laugh because I tried to stop this stupid wedding?"

"They will laugh at your arriving bound and gagged," Madame said.

"You mean you will tell people?" Rose Henriette demanded. "Then no more custom from me. And I shall tell my friends—"

Madame Ferrier regretted this. But she said, "What if it gets to the ears of the Marquis of Flynte's mother, the dear Duchess? A lady of the old school. A rigid disciplinarian, I understand. An adherent of a stricter regime. But what a beautiful country seat they have. When the Marquis inherits—"

Rose Henriette looked as if she could have killed her.

"Robert—" Julian murmured.

Robert kissed me again, straightened his jacket, smoothed down his hair and entered the church with his friend. Jamie followed and Sarah Drew and Mrs Jarrett.

Madame Ferrier untied the scarves from Miss Hatton's ankles and wrists. Madame tidied her up and dusted her down. In anger, I thought Rose Henriette handsome, not merely pretty. Then, with a hand on her arm, Madame guided Miss Hatton to the church porch. There she herself put the lace shawl over Rose Henriette's yellow curls which were in enchanting disarray.

They went inside, the hand still on Miss Hatton's elbow, a hand which could turn to a grip of iron in a second, I thought.

"Eccentricity," I heard Mr Dee say, forgivingly, since it was the rich Hattons who were eccentric.

"They are brushed with it," I murmured and heard Emmeline laugh.

In the church porch, she looked me up and down. "You are perfect," she said. "Now, one last kiss for Martha Bates. I thank God every night, my love, for your friendship."

"Do not make me weep now," I implored.

"Weep?" she echoed. "With Robert waiting?"

I walked decorously up the aisle on Mr Dee's arm but I gave my ear-rings one small shake to feel them.

Madame Ferrier and Rose Henriette sat at the back of the church. She, who was to be my sister-in-law soon, did not look up as I passed. Madame gave me a small smile. You have been almost a mother to me, I thought.

Jamie, fair, tall, handsome, smiled at me. Those matrons, Mrs Drew and Mrs Jarrett, looked serious as befitted the occasion. I wondered, though, if Mrs Jarrett thought of that reprobate, her husband, and even here in this place gave thanks that he had gone before.

Such wonderful friends, I marvelled again.

Family? I would not dwell on this. I would build our family, Robert's and mine. Do not look back, I told myself. You are walking towards your future, step by step, towards Robert who is waiting for you, as Emmeline says.

I suppose my mother-in-law would be coldly polite to me. My father-in-law was an enigma. I did not know what kind of gentleman he was. But I would try to make friends with him while never going so far as to substitute making wimples for creating bonnets; Rose Henriette might, for the sake of face, outwardly accept, easier for her if she was, say, the Marchioness of Flynte to Arabella's plain Mrs Comstock.

Now I was beside Robert. He had remarked, more than once, upon my smile, so now I smiled at him and with all my love. I hoped he understood. I was certain he did. In the smile he must have recognized that now and for ever he was all my world.

FREE
Fawcett Books Listing

There is Romance, Mystery, Suspense, and Adventure waiting for you inside the Fawcett Books Order Form. And it's yours to browse through and use to get all the books you've been wanting . . . but possibly couldn't find in your bookstore.

This easy-to-use order form is divided into categories and contains over 1500 titles by your favorite authors.

So don't delay—take advantage of this special opportunity to increase your reading pleasure.

Just send us your name and address and 35¢ (to help defray postage and handling costs).